CW00346781

In a State of Memory

Latin American Women Writers

Series Editors

JEAN FRANCO
Columbia University

FRANCINE MASIELLO
University of California at Berkeley

TUNUNA MERCADO

MARY LOUISE PRATT
Stanford University

TUNUNA MERCADO

In a State of Memory

Translated by Peter Kahn

With an introduction by

Jean Franco

University of
Nebraska Press

Lincoln & London

Publication of this book was assisted by a grant
from the National Endowment for the Arts.

Originally published as *En estado de memoria*
© 1990 by Tununa Mercado

Translation and introduction
© 2001 by the University of Nebraska Press
All rights reserved

Manufactured in the United States
of America

Library of Congress Cataloging-in-Publication Data
Mercado, Tununa, 1939–
[En estado de memoria. English]
In a state of memory / Tununa Mercado ; translated by Peter Kahn ;
with an introduction by Jean Franco.
p.   cm. — (Latin American women writers)
ISBN 0-8032-3157-1 (cloth : alk. paper) —
ISBN 0-8032-8269-9 (pbk. : alk. paper)
I. Title. II. Series.
PQ7798.23.E7197 E64 2001
863'.64—dc21   00-064836

In memory of
Mario Usabiaga

this is a book
about relentless
anxiety.

Contents

Translator's Preface ix

Introduction by Jean Franco xiii

1 The Illness 1

2 The Cold That Never Comes 18

3 Poor Person's Body 28

4 Curriculum Vitae 41

5 Oracles 47

6 The Order of the Day 55

7 Emissary 60

8 Cellular Chambers 65

9 The Furtive Species 73

10 The Guided Visit 82

11 Houses 91

12 Embassy 96

13 Container 101

14 Phenomenology 108

15 Exposure 116

16 The Wall 142

[vii]

Translator's Preface

Tununa Mercado, born in the province of Córdoba, Argentina, now lives in Buenos Aires. During two periods of military dictatorship (1966–70, 1974–86) she lived in exile, first in France and then in Mexico. Here, in this book, through flashbacks, recollections, and short personal narratives, she confronts the exile experience, including one of the most difficult and complex aspects: the conclusion of the journey and the return to her native country.

Tununa maintains a powerful presence in Argentine culture today. She is active in the national literary scene, she is a vocal spokesperson for feminist issues, and she enters occasionally in public debates about political issues. Above all, Tununa is identified as a champion of literary style. Her attention to detail, narrative tone, and wry sincerity are elements of her literary technique that attracted me to this project and combined to make it both a pleasure and a challenge. Together, Tununa and I have done our best to conserve and transfer this stunning piece of autobiographical fiction into the English language.

Translator's Preface

As suggested by the title, *In a State of Memory* addresses a subject that is particularly troubling in all countries whose historical memory has been deformed by dictatorship. Rather than present a "factual" version of the past, Tununa explores the lapses and distortions that occur both during exile and upon return from exile. Her particular vision of this experience is a blend of perplexity, humor, and alienation. The events described in this book, whether factual or not, form part of both the individual and collective experience; the violence of separation from one's homeland produces a vacuum in the life of the protagonist as well as in the flow of life for an entire nation, and this book represents an effort by one person to confront and fill that void.

I first met Tununa Mercado, fittingly, in a university building in the center of Buenos Aires, two blocks from the Plaza de Mayo. The building was, and still is, in a state of distressing disrepair, though vestiges of its former splendor remain. This contrast between Argentina's past and present is a frequent preoccupation for Tununa, both in her writing and, as I discovered, in her daily life and conversation. Working with Tununa on this translation involved numerous meetings highlighted by a wealth of anecdotes and recollections that could easily be transformed into yet another book.

The thrill of working with a writer while translating her work lies not only in being granted the freedom to ask questions and receive willing responses but in catching those responses in unguarded moments: the writer's response to a phrase, a scene, or a person, even before she actually speaks; her eyes or her posture, a smile or a frown. Often a query is answered in the absence of words, the response embodied by a gesture, a furtive glance, a simple sigh.

Translator's Preface

The joy of translating and, for that matter, reading is the voyage one embarks upon beyond the words. It is a voyage into a world of infinite possibilities—for every translation is different from every other—and, of course, it is a struggle against impossibility, the hopelessness of translating an idea from one language to another, unless these ideas can, in some way, come to feel as if they belong to you also. In this sense, Tununa became my teacher. As reading and translating her book was a novel experience for me, she made me feel that our work together was also a novel experience for her, an undertaking to which she was firmly committed. My questions sometimes caused new ideas to spring to mind—whether they had anything to do, really, with the book itself—and in this sharing of fresh views and impressions, through our combined efforts, a work has emerged, a work of translation that I hope will be as enjoyable and enlightening to read as it was to work on.

The process of translation is always a journey into and beyond the words and world of a writer. In this case, the experience could not have been more fulfilling and illuminating. After numerous succulent lunches, countless coffees, and long conversations since our first meeting in that singular building in the heart of Buenos Aires, I am very pleased that this book is finally going to appear in English for more readers to discover and appreciate.

Introduction

Jean Franco

" Legend has it that we were descended from an Indian prin-
cess, the daughter of Chief Quechuden, otherwise known
as Lechibán, which means 'Sunlight,' and with whom
our ancestor Baigorria—a name that in Basque means the 'highest part of the meadow'—had sons and daughters. He also had
them with a creole wife,[1] but my family wanted us to be descended from a family of Ranquel Indians because they believed
that the true Argentine aristocracy was of pure autochthonous
origins." So writes Tunuña Mercado in her memoir, *La madriguera*.[2] She was born in Córdoba, Argentina, in 1939. Her
father, a lawyer and politician was a conservative in the Córdoba
manner, "that is to say, he had his anti-clerical and progressive

1. "Creole," derived in English from Caribbean usage, is not a translation
of "criollo," which in Argentine means an American-born but non-indigenous
inhabitant.

2. Tunuña Mercado, *La madriguera* (Buenos Aires: Tusquets Editores,
1996). Translation mine.

Introduction

side."[3] He also possessed an excellent library and a mordant wit, which his daughter inherited.

She married her literature professor, Noe Jitrik, in 1961, before graduating from university. For three years she lived in Besançon, France, where her husband was visiting professor at the university, and just before moving there, she published her first collection of short stories, *Celebrar a la mujer como a una pascua*, in 1967.

After her return to Buenos Aires in 1970, she began work as a journalist on Jacobo Timerman's newspaper, *La Opinión*. This was one of the most intense moments of Argentine history. There were riots in Córdoba, guerrilla actions, kidnappings, and assassinations. When the Peronists won a victory in the elections of 1973, many people placed their hopes on the return of the exiled Perón, whom they expected to heal the divided country. His arrival at Ezeiza airport in that year was a portent of things to come. The right-wing Peronists opened fire on the left-wing Peronist youth, killing a number of them, and in the following months Perón was unable to hold together the warring factions of his party. When he died in 1974, his widow, Isabel, became president, but by then it was clear that the military was ready to seize power and "restore order" as it had already done in neighboring Chile. The repressive nature of the new state rapidly became apparent, and Mercado's husband, a prominent literary and political figure, received death threats. With her family, Mercado left for Mexico. During her twelve-year period of exile, she studied weaving, wrote art criticism, served on the

3. Tununa Mercado, "Crisol de razas en patio cordobés," in *La letra de lo minimo*, (Buenos Aires: Beatriz Viterbo, 1994), pp. 9–13.

feminist journal *fem,* and was active in Argentine exile organizations. Soon after her return to Argentina in 1986, she published a collection of stories, *Canon de alcoba* (1988), and a novel, *En estado de memoria* (1990; *In a State of Memory*), which are only now beginning to receive the critical attention they deserve.

In his book *The Untimely Present,* the Brazilian critic Idelber Avelar writes that *In a State of Memory* "narrates the conditions of possibility for writing after a catastrophe." [4] The catastrophe in question was the "dirty war" waged by the Argentine military against the civilian population between 1976 and 1982. Under the pretext of an anti-communist crusade, the military used the cruelest of tactics—"disappearing" thousands of people, sending some prisoners to their death from the air, torturing and executing others in the death camps, and giving the babies of victims to military families for adoption. Twenty years after the collapse of the military government, and after President Alfonsín's government declared a full stop to the trials of members of the military, the dirty war is still an open wound, particularly for families and descendants of the disappeared.

In 1984, the report of the National Comission on the Disappearance of People, *Nunca Más (Never Again),* commented that "the enormity of what had happened, the transgression of the very foundations of the species" [5] stretched the limits of the believable. For although the military had also taken over in Chile,

---

4. Idelber Avelar, *The Untimely Present: Postdictatorial Latin American Fiction and the Task of Mourning* (Durham NC: Duke University Press, 1999), p. 228.

5. Comisión Nacional sobre la Desaparición de Personas, *Nunca Más: Informe de La Comisión Nacional sobre la Desaparición de Personas* (Buenos Aires: EUDEBA, 1984), p. 15.

Introduction

Uruguay, and Brazil, the perversity of the Argentine repressive apparatus exceeded those in the other states of the Southern Cone. Thirty thousand people disappeared and died in the death camps. During the military regime, mothers of the disappeared, known as the Mothers of the Plaza de Mayo, courageously demonstrated every Thursday to break the silence over the disappearances, but it was not until the restoration of democracy that the full extent of the historical trauma began to be grasped. Human rights groups, including the Grandmothers of the Plaza de Mayo, the Children of the Disappeared, and the Mothers of the Plaza de Mayo, refused to let matters drop: they identified torturers and marked their homes. The Grandmothers searched for the adopted children of the disappeared and brought in forensic experts to identify bones in the excavated grave sites. But though memory and amnesia have entered and at times dominated the political vocabulary, expediency has tended to gloss over the deeper problems of how to arrive at historical truth or whether there can be *a* historical truth. The tendency to commute individual memory too rapidly into social or collective memory means that it can be monumentalized in ways that frustrate the complexities. And it is precisely here in this intersection between the subject and the social that Tununa Mercado's remarkable and uncompromising novel *In a State of Memory* is situated.

Written as a first person narrative of exile and return, it is both memoir and novel, a text that is difficult to classify, for although the protagonist is clearly identifiable as Mercado herself, a referential reading is the least illuminating approach. It is a deeply philosophical not to say ethical work examining intricate states of consciousness in a way that is rare in Latin American literature, in which inner states are rarely probed and never in

Introduction

such detail or with such subtlety. It is a sustained account of mental and physical symptoms beyond the immediate reality of exile that exposes the very condition of personhood.

In the opening pages, the anonymous narrator is waiting for her turn at the psychiatric clinic when Cindal bursts into the waiting room in great distress from an ulcer, howling with pain and pleading to be committed. "The patients, assembled in the waiting room for problems that were quite minor compared to Cindal's terminal situation, were frozen, gripped by his shrieks and howls." The psychoanalyst refuses to change the schedule, and that night Cindal hangs himself. "Cindal, whose name returns to my memory with regularity, always with the stress on the letter *i*, whose twisted posture appears over and over, was left to die because his demands could not be answered, and because demands of that nature do nothing but interfere with the lives of others and undermine the plenitude to which everyone has a right." It is these demands "that could not be answered" with which the novel engages. It is as if the skin of fantasy that protects most of us from recognition of the real—that is, of death and mortality—is missing, leaving the protagonist permanently exposed to the horror of everyday life. By "real" I mean that fundamental human condition for which there is no cure and that institutions seek to cover over with the veil of normalcy. Psychiatry with its promise of a cure is the principal offender. In the course of the novel, the narrator even extracts some bitter humor from her various unsuccessful visits to psychiatrists not to mention all kinds of other healers. In one of her psychiatric sessions she is unable to utter a word, and "not one manifestation of the unconscious slipped out, not one dream." In another session, with a friend who combined Freudian psycho-

Introduction

analysis, Zen Buddhism, and the way of Tao, she finally confesses that what she wants is to write, but she is baffled when the psychiatrist suggests she take a job in advertising. From such frustrated encounters she often emerges with physical symptoms that her psychiatrists vainly attempt to interpret, and when no explanation is forthcoming, they refer her, "from one set of hands to another, from one ear to another, from the couch to the chair, with fluctuating interpretations of the symptoms: mistaking rigidity for hysteria, neurological disorder for returning to the womb, incontinence for attention-winning strategies, and so on." Clearly this is a woman for whom the given world is intolerable, a woman who cannot deal with competition, tests, evaluations, and the countless ways in which one individual is pitted against another to test his or her social worth. Her defense when she is forced into one of these situations is evasion, self-effacement, and refusal. It is not that she is antisocial but rather that the "social"—interpellating, as it does, a sovereign subject—is quite alien to her. Everything in her life suggests a flight from individuation. Her work as a ghost writer—correcting other people's prose, infiltrating her own ideas into another's writing—is anonymous, never publicly acknowledged. Her clothing and furniture are second-hand, as if she cannot exercise those privileges of individualism: choice and taste. Indeed, this condition of self-effacement applies to Tununa Mercado herself, as seen on the cover of Argentine editions of *En estado de memoria,* with their gray and black colors that fade into the background beside the bold red, orange, and blue book jackets favored by the book trade.

Exile does not altogether account for this extreme state of alienation expressed in the book. On a return visit to Argentina at

Introduction

the end of the military dictatorship, the narrator revisits her old school and encounters a schoolteacher who is exactly as she remembers her. But the encounter brings back the memory of her first day in class when the other children fell into line in the schoolyard and she discovered that there was no assigned place for her. Even in those days she knew she was not on the rolls, not inscribed in the social text.

So exile exacerbates a condition that is already latent, the more so because it is a period of suspense that disregards the flow of time. Reports of death and disappearance are inescapable; there are the daily telephone calls, the newspaper reports, the atrocity stories of new arrivals. "We almost always dream of death," she writes, using the collective pronoun while casting doubts onto the possibility of a collective experience. True, there is the common experience of second-hand existence: "We lived by proxy, through third parties, struggling with the memory of a country that was a thousand kilometers away and transporting it to the barrios of Aguilas and Tlacopac." But the collective "we" turns out to be as illusory as those endless meetings and discussions, for she and her comrades construct a "political cathedral, without territorial foundations," a structure that disappears as soon as the military government falls and the exiles return. What might for others have constituted a community among exiles is for her an expenditure of energy that cannot be a foundation for the future.

Nor can the narrator take refuge in memory as if it offered some translatable lesson or meaning. Memory is, for her, so intimately bound up with particularities—a gesture, a casual remark that sticks in the mind, some seemingly unimportant everyday activity like grilling a steak—that it becomes inscribed as

Introduction

habitus but on no account can it be commuted into social or collective memory. Is there such a thing as a common or shared memory? In an attempt to understand what the return from exile might eventually mean for her, she visits the village in Asturias, Spain, where her friend the exile Ovidio Gondi was raised, and she finally tracks down a woman who remembers his father. She is shown a photograph of a field with a cross that marks the site where the father had been executed three years after Franco took power. But this experience that she carefully stores in her memory cannot be passed on to Gondi himself, who declares, "Everything is unreal and that's how it remains in one's memory."

Can history mean anything if it does not become part of individual memory? In Mexico, along with her family (who are always in the background but rarely present in the narrative) she spends Sundays visiting the house in Coyoacan where Trotsky was murdered, which is now a museum of books, furniture, and memorabilia. The visits do not clarify the historical event or convert her to Trotsky's political cause but rather have the effect of absorbing this public figure into private family mythology.

On her return to Buenos Aires, she revisits the streets and buildings of her earlier life, often without recognizing them, or fictionalizing scenes that had never happened. And though one might imagine that here, finally, she would experience some closure or find some sense of community, the *polis* continues to evade her. She joins the Mothers of the Plaza de Mayo in their Thursday demonstrations, meeting women who have lost entire families in the repression. But of course she is not one of them, and as the days pass so does the concept of the community of the *polis* as the place of achievable justice fade away.

Introduction

As we read Mercado's prose, her precision and care for detail make us aware of how gross is the language normally employed to describe states of consciousness. For even self-conscious literary language often compartmentalizes the senses and secures the boundaries of individuation. While some writers try to invent a new language, Mercado creates a new image of consciousness. At one point, she describes a "cellular chamber," "a secret factory, a compartment outside the flow of the five senses but spanning and subsuming them all through condensations as yet lacking nomenclature." It is this supplementary compartment that is both the place of terror where one faces the possible destruction of the self and the place that nourishes imagination. What she discovers when she dares to penetrate "the forbidden zones of my memory" is not the memory of herself but an old photograph of concentration camps with masses of anonymous bodies, open graves, a Nazi parade. For what is deeply recessed in memory is a holocaust and perhaps the shared responsibility of all humanity in the atrocity. For this photograph is, in its way, an image of "community," a collectivity in which the individual (whether buried in the mass grave or lined up in the ranks of the military) has been obliterated. One asks whether for Mercado there can be an "excluded middle" as Gillian Rose calls it,[6] between the libertarian or individualist society and the totalitarian community. Not that Mercado puts it in these terms. Her narrator can only make tentative efforts from the depths of her own solitude to establish some minimal contact with the other. In the first weeks of her return to Argen-

---

6. Gillian Rose, *Mourning Becomes the Law: Philosophy and Representation* (Cambridge: Cambridge University Press, 1996), pp. 4–5.

tina, she becomes obsessed by a homeless man lying on a park bench exposed to the weather. He is said to have suffered a trauma that makes him shun the normal props of everyday life—the daily news, shelter, friendship. She tries to establish contact with him, only to realize that though his condition seems to reflect her own "exposure," there is no commonality in their different solitudes.

Retreating into her study, she sits facing a high wall that blocks out the view of the city and on which she begins to write. But she will not emerge from this Platonic cave with absolute knowledge, nor is it the kind of self-discovery that we often encounter in women's writing in which, after the trials of growing up, the girl finally puts pen to paper and thus arrives at a consciousness of her own personhood. For the narrator here, still less does it lead to the self-forgetfulness that occurs when she is weaving. Writing is far less benevolent an experience: in it "one only encounters misfortune; and not misfortune as a personal sentiment, but as an expression of fundamental nudity: not knowing, the inability to fill the void or approach the universal." The "void" is greater than the historical trauma. It is not something with which one comes to terms or which can be healed. Indeed, that she spent months in a reading group in Mexico pouring over Hegel's *Phenomenology of Mind* without attaining some final grasp of the matter is symptomatic, for if we are to believe Slavoj Žižek, "far from being a story of the progressive overcoming, dialectics is for Hegel a systematic notion of the failure of all such attempts."[7] There is always something that escapes the words on the page.

7. Slavoj Žižek, *The Sublime Object of Ideology* (London: Verso, 1989), p. 6.

Introduction

The wall, "her doom and incitement," her "witness-wall," "a hurdle" between herself and her "descent back to earth," is an accident of construction that blocks her view while it reflects light before sinking into darkness. On its surfaces are traces like hieroglyphs that beg to be deciphered. And it is on this surface that she finally begins to write, not in a linear progression but by forming small nuclei of writing, with overlapping texts, until overloaded with writing, the wall slips down "like a sheet of paper sliding vertically into a slot." The ending is both enigmatic and visionary, neither cure nor solution, and like all major works of fiction, the novel as a whole raises questions rather than proposing solutions. It is devoutly to be hoped that this translation will make this extraordinary and subtle work available to a wider public.

Mercado's short fictions in *Canón de alcoba* are not yet available in English, but they are just as extraordinary. They have often been described as erotic texts, although this is only true if we extend the term "erotic" beyond its banal associations to include the prose itself, which could almost be described as luxurious. These vignettes are sometimes descriptions of a witnessed event—a man exposing himself on a subway train in such a way that all the people on the subway car have their attention fixed on his penis, or a busy marketplace in which the buyers are distracted by a mutilated man's hook appearing like a periscope through a grating—sometimes they are dreamlike, as in her description of riderless horses galloping through the countryside. She herself has described her preference for "minimal writing," in other words, writing that attends to such details as those registered by the senses. What she achieves is the perfection she finds in the humble act of sewing in which "there is no margin

Introduction

for error: to sew, stitch, embroider is to approach perfection, no less. Tautologically one might say that anyone who does not do it perfectly had better leave the needle aside and try something else, just as the person who can't sing should accept silence."[8]

8. Tununa Mercado, *Canón de alcoba* (Buenos Aires: Ada Korn, 1988), p. 170.

In a State of Memory

The Illness

The name Cindal, whose spelling escapes me, comes back to me time and again along with a man and the words of that man incessantly repeated in the waiting room of a psychiatric clinic. *Tell him to do something for me, please! Tell him to do something for me! I have an ulcer! I have an ulcer!* he cried, not a little repetitively. While he begged and pleaded, I imagined a factory in some part of his body, at the pit of his stomach judging from the way he was doubled over, clutching at his waist, in some part of his body where ulcers were bursting without remission or pity. The patients, assembled in the waiting room for problems that were quite minor compared to Cindal's terminal situation, were frozen, gripped by his shrieks and howls. The receptionist, to whom Cindal appealed to see the doctor, had no idea how to deal with the unusual case that had barged into the office with no prior phone call, no appointment, and no previous visits, but that nonetheless did not seem a violent man. She disappeared toward the interior of the clinic and reappeared with the message that the doctor could not attend to him, that he was presently in a session, and that he would see the scheduled group in the waiting room next. The man then approached and pleaded with us, in a voice trembling with suffering, to grant him a few minutes of our hour. But the hour was sacred, and although we were willing to surrender some terrain of our madness so that he could unburden himself of his own, the psychiatrist was adamant: he would not see him.

One is so helpless in the hands of psychiatrists as to be incapable of even questioning their dictates; one comes to suppose that, in the presumed transferential submission, the doctor may have chosen an effective therapeutic tactic when deciding to *set* a desperate and unscheduled patient *straight*. He wanted to set Cindal straight, to make him see that he could not simply manipulate his own madness, nor other people's time; so, finally, Cindal went away, though not without pleading once more to be admitted to the hospital: *Please, commit me!* The psychiatrist, once in his office, maintained a strict silence and would not respond to a single one of our questions; I understand that over time psychiatrists have perfected this analytical, beyond-the-grave silence insofar as anyone desperate for immediate answers is concerned. Cindal hanged himself that very night.

I cannot stop thinking about Cindal. Who might have mourned him, who mourns him still; I wonder who other than I remembers him, doubled over in pain, pitiful, suffering his ulcer the way one does daily chores, the way one does schoolwork, in the waiting room of death, tracing resplendent red letters with the blood seeping from the wounds of his ulcer, bleeding internally and finally departing, dragging himself to the other world, drowned in his own blood. He would get up, I suppose, in the morning or at night, or after a short daytime nap during which he may have succeeded in subduing his pain, he would awaken and find himself yet again with the ulcer, not a solitary, isolated ulcer but one in permanent communication with his mind, as if it were all one and the same thing, the ulcer and the terror, the terror unleashed by the ulcer, or the ulcer unleashed by the terror. Ulcer and terror were inseparable for Cindal during those sleepless hours of his day. He would double over and howl, pleading for help.

People like that who suffer with such conviction—this was said after Cindal had hung himself from a rope—must be left alone, nothing can be done for them; and when such people seek and find their own death, it is commonly agreed that they have found peace, that they have gently slipped away, and that, in the end, they have ceased to suffer. Cindal was left to die because it was thought that death was what he really wanted and that sooner or later he was going to have his way. Cindal, whose name returns to my memory with regularity, always with the stress on the letter *i,* whose twisted posture appears over and over, was left to die because his demands could not be answered and because demands of that nature do nothing but interfere with the lives of others and undermine the plenitude to which everyone has a right. No one who lives his or her life in conformity, replete with projects and certainties, no one who enjoys life's constant gratifications, can let down their guard and permit people like Cindal to enter their world, a person who did not make appointments, who did not book passages, and who even arrived late, at the final tattered shreds of the sanity that a psychiatrist's couch might have offered him.

Cindal's name often sprang to mind when I found myself in situations similar to the one he had endured, imploringly, in the psychiatrist's waiting room. There is a vast difference, however, between his demands and mine. He seemed determined to proclaim his at the top of his lungs, as if all restraint had abandoned him and there was nothing left to hide his self-pity. He could no longer control his entreaties, he had fallen to his knees in genuflection, bent over, no sense of pride could halt his most certain end. While I, on the other hand, obstinately postpone any outburst of anguish, partly due to my good upbringing, not wishing to ruin anyone else's party, employing any number of stratagems in an effort to disguise the agonizing peaks of the affliction that assaults me. I would find it so very difficult to expose my affliction, to disappoint those around me, to have them see that the poem's ancient "force that through the green fuse drives the flower, drives my green age . . ." was, in fact, the perfect incubator for ulcers and gastritis, and to throw away the tranquility with which they watched me while away the hours and the days would have served no purpose at all.

In strict therapeutic terms, psychoanalysis has never been very generous to me. To be perfectly honest, I never had access to any individual and horizontal clinical treatment where I could spill the material of my unconscious mind; for financial reasons, I always had to attend group sessions in which I succeeded, with little effort, in concealing my anguish and vulnerability from my companions as well as, perhaps, from the sagacity of the psychiatrist; I managed to share in the collective laughter or tears, aided by my good manners and a certain sense of the ridiculous that, because of its cynicism, might better be described as bitterness.

So, I never received any individualized attention through which I might have discerned my conflicts in a specialized and specific way; no psychiatrist ever concerned himself with me in particular, thus leaving my immense capacity for transference without outlet other than the various forms of dependence on doctors of all kinds, including dentists, gynecologists, and, above all, faith healers of the most varied species: witch doctors, shamans, and "masters," all of whom endeavored to cleanse my body. Using sprigs of mint and basil, censers of myrrh and incense, garlic cloves, lotions, coconut shells, oracles, and other techniques of chance, they tried to cure me of my ailments and save me from evil spells, and indeed at times they succeeded, for there cannot exist a more fertile ground for such cures than my poor body and soul.

In 1967, seven days after the death of Che Guevara, which so radically devastated our lives, and just before I was to embark on a trip to France for an extended stay, that same psychiatrist I have already mentioned, who had me in his group for three years and who so mercilessly dispensed with Cindal, seeing that I might founder in my transatlantic trajectory, allotted several hours of individual attention to me, during which I failed to utter a single word; alone, without the crutch of the group, I fell silent, I had nothing to say to my analyst, not one manifestation of the unconscious slipped out, not one dream, and he too remained silent during those two or three sessions, without my ever finding out what his evaluation of my psychiatric condition was, or whether through his silence he had condemned or absolved me, or if he simply had nothing to say; but in fact, sensing that I might not have the strength to survive the approaching changes, he gave me the address of a Swiss psychiatrist who spoke Spanish as a result of having lived and worked in Argentina; he told me that he was going to correspond with her on my behalf, and I went so far as to imagine that he was going to send along my diagnosis; the idea that I might have an existence as a *case* calmed me down a bit: my health, or my mental illness, had assumed a singular character. And it is not inappropriate to speak of a mental illness since it was constantly impressed upon us during our therapy sessions that we were there as mental patients.

Once in France, realizing that I was indeed in no condition to bear up under such a "change," a euphemism used to designate a critical moment, I wrote the promised letter to the Swiss psychoanalyst the very day after my arrival. I wasted no time; having barely unpacked my suitcases and those of my family, I began to write the letter in which I explained that until recently I had been the patient of doctor so-and-so and that he, for his part, would be writing soon regarding my case and that I wanted to meet with her to begin treatment. I suggested biweekly sessions and explained that I was living scarcely a hundred kilometers from Geneva, where she had her clinic, and that my idea was to make an initial trip just to review my sufferings with her. The letter was written, of course, in Spanish, not only because she had command of that language but also because I did not speak a word of French. I only knew how to recite a fragment of *Nausea,* by Sartre, which I had often read aloud and even committed to memory in the French class I attended for two weeks before leaving Buenos Aires. I was almost tempted to transcribe the fragment in order to illustrate the anguish I was in, but I did not: the mere act of sending the letter, of setting my sights on a therapeutic goal, made me feel better. And so extreme is my therapeutic disposition, and so inveterate, that once the letter was sent, at that precise instant, I placed all my hopes on Switzerland.

It was a cruel beginning to winter, very cruel; the roads were covered with snow, and I was aware that the trip between Besançon and Geneva could be plagued with misadventures. I envisaged traveling through frozen forests on white trains, traversing white countries, and I felt a sudden rush of panic that could only be eased by thoughts of my imminent cure; I was going to cross over the iced landscape, but the ice was not going to break beneath my feet—I was not going to get my tail wet, like the fox in the *I Ching* during his winter journey—because I was going to have individual, prolonged, radicalized psychiatric treatment.

I never had the opportunity to test the ice; Madame Spira, who, judging by her fame, might well have been psychoanalyst to Queen Juliana, could not "for the moment" take on a biweekly commitment; her hours were all taken. There was no mention in her letter of having received my *case* from Buenos Aires, no letter had forwarded me to her adoptive care, no reference to my psychoanalyst at all; she said she was at my service for some future time, asked me to excuse her, and, meanwhile, remained sincerely mine. Her answer did not surprise me: I had already realized that the feat of paying for analysis in Swiss francs, trips that would involve winding through mountains and bordering cliffs, paid in Swiss francs, weekly lodging near or far from Lake Geneva, paid in Swiss francs, all of this had, for several weeks now, seemed rather laughable and disproportionate, a poor person's fantasy. Once again, I had failed in my attempt to obtain a profound, individual treatment, of the sort to which thousands of Argentine women and men had gained rightful access over the last thirty years.

I have always contented myself with surrogate treatments. Upon my return to Argentina after that stay in France, for example, the same psychoanalyst who had put me in contact with Madame Spira, without the least idea of the outlandishness of his proposal, referred me to another one of his colleagues, this time a local one who, once again, given my financial situation, placed me in group therapy. Now, my very first experience of group analysis had involved hallucinogens. And every time I have related this experience succinctly and almost truthfully, my listeners have tended to assume a rather deadpan expression that, more than indifference, betrayed a decision to maintain a certain distance from a budding danger of contagion; when I say that we dropped acid, psilocybin, or mescaline, fearsome names that they are, they prefer not to listen; rather, they scrutinize me for signs of lasting damage.

The fact is that such therapy with psychotropic drugs was no longer in vogue when I went to my new psychoanalyst; after the coup of '66, these treatments were first questioned and then forbidden: for ideological or moral reasons, and uncritically confusing psychiatric uses with drug dependency, they discarded, without having made any progress, a technique that induced hallucinations. Abandoning ourselves to the effects of chemicals, we had taken flight toward our points of origin, not, of course, without a very high cost at the moment, because anyone who supposes that these kinds of incursions produce pleasure, unadulterated pleasure, is quite mistaken: the emotional upheaval provoked by a return to any such point of origin—be it the maternal uterus, the bastion of the species, the echo of the primal orphan scream, or any such thing—is not to be wished on anyone, and only because we had been convinced of the medical nature of these practices did the group give in to and accept the risk of losing or winning everything in a single session.

Given that it was no longer possible to take peyote or psilocybin, and without anyone thinking to question the law that prohibited it, the group would gather around the psychoanalyst without the benefits of acid, exposed only to the effects of her bird-woman stare. Upon leaving her office, we would go to one or another of our houses to smoke hashish or some other flower bud that might serve as an acid substitute. On one of those occasions I puffed a bit too enthusiastically on the joint, and by the time I got home my head was so splintered that when I wanted to say *I,* I said *she,* and I had to beg them to piece me back together, to restore me to my niche, my dwelling place previous to that moment of reckless unselfconsciousness; but it was not easy returning me to myself, or uprooting me from myself, or gaining access to that *other* of whom I could catch only glimpses, or snaring that *additional other* who would not let me go, and I could not distinguish between that other who had to be driven away and that other who was mine and had to be retained.

In spite of the dearth of palliatives that psychoanalysis offered me, a sort of plumbing of my inner depths, I never ceased delivering myself to its *manes.* In the throes of exile, when every day some fresh, horrible piece of news arrived from Argentina, and often it came to us via telephone calls from just about anywhere on earth, including our native land, and frequently we were told of the murder of someone, or of several, or of a particularly close friend of ours, almost family, or of two or three who had shared with me and my loved ones some form of bond, in those cruelest of moments when one could do nothing but sit on the edge of the bed and cry, to live was to survive. But one of those days the burden got to be too much, a day when the aura of death to which we were subjected was too present and immediate, and I felt my health begin to crumble. The spasms of gastritis, which would later occur with severity, were at that time

The Illness

barely a diffuse pain in the pit of my stomach, a vague sensation similar to that which lingers after receiving an accidental blow while roughhousing as a child. Mostly my afflictions were concentrated in my throat, which obstinately incubated a host of inflammations and blisters that were resistant to all antibiotics. Hardened like tar, the mucous membrane rigid and slippery, the glands swollen, not one cilium vibrating with the passage of air or the sound of my voice, coated with an extensive colony of golden bacteria, my throat, it seemed, was the site at which my own death was being engendered.

Suffering cramps in my neck and an incipient septicemia, my end was almost surely drawing near; I went to doctors, clinics, and laboratories and was subjected to all kinds of tests; in vain I poured my blood into test tubes and sent my liquids away to be cultured; nothing happened, the cure passed me by without so much as a nod. If my life had been painted as a retable, I would have appeared on my sickbed in a room so filled with fever that the ceiling would bulge, the window on the wall would have the curtains drawn back to allow the light of the Holy Spirit to enter: the scene of a miracle, of rejuvenation by a luminous, unearthly light. A legend would caption the miracle cure: "When all hope of keeping her alive had been lost, she was commended to the Virgin and cured by her Grace in the last days of October in the year of our Lord, nineteen-hundred-seventy-six." The feat was really the doing of a homeopath and the result of a remedy of Marigold 1-30, diluted in a glass of water and ingested at half-hour intervals at first, then once every hour, and, finally, three times per day.

I was lucky because no one ventured to suggest that my problem was psychological; it was accepted as something natural that

The Illness

I should go to a medical doctor. When other people living in exile complained of a loss of energy, they were told that such symptoms were to be expected, that depression was the logical outcome of having been uprooted from one's home, particularly after so many losses and so much terror and pain endured in Argentina. They were advised to see a psychoanalyst who, as was customary, adhered to the political convictions of whatever group they belonged to. This analyst, to whom the recently arrived would entrust themselves, was most likely to stick to his sphere of training and not recommend laboratory tests, holding true to his particular ideas regarding depression, in which case the organism would play dirty tricks on itself, and the illness would continue its evolution, discouraging both the analyst and the patient; the analyst would *refer* his patient elsewhere, a poorly considered course of action whose consequence was, in effect, nothing more than a referral from one set of hands to another, from one ear to another, from the couch to the chair, with fluctuating interpretations of the symptoms: mistaking rigidity for hysteria, neurological disorder for returning to the womb, incontinence for attention-winning strategies, and so on.

One spends an entire lifetime trying to find support, trying to make the paltry psychic mass stick to external structures in an effort to give them some kind of shape; one seeks the society of others, be they persons, animals, or things, to fuse oneself to them; one adopts habits hoping, through repetition, to avoid unhappiness. Our resources are inexhaustible and renewable day by day; at times they operate like incantations, ingenuous vows that hour after hour are deposited upon small domestic altars and for which we hope to receive compensation. If there is a full moon, for example, one closes the window so as to impede the exacerbation of the madness produced by its rays; and if the wind howls, one closes the window to bar the entry of its demons; if, however, a bird sings, one turns an attentive ear so that the benefit of its trill may penetrate. A person is in permanent relation to the external world; whatever intrudes from the other side of the wall conditions one's movements and orders one's rituals; a person strives, fundamentally, to be part of a group, to belong to the flock, supposing with good reason that this belonging might provide distance from madness or, at least, from uncertainty.

What I had to lay out before a psychiatrist or, on another level or to a different degree, to a psychoanalyst was a series of nuclei that would not disappear. They were, or are, states of helplessness, a frailty when facing daily events; I had to explain to the analyst that any *competitive* situation provoked in me an imperious need to flee and avoid engaging in battle; if the confrontation centered upon my merits, the impulse to erase myself from the battlefield would become an inextinguishable focus of all my anxieties; as if by defining my capabilities in order to gain a position, I also put my very existence on trial.

I could never compete for positions very well, and if by some twist of fate I was ever positively appraised, the evaluation was not the product of a contest in which I was selected as one among many, but, perhaps, thereafter or as an aside, as if it were only through an afterthought that my merits were discovered. Brilliance unperceived or brilliance imperceptible to others were some of the interpretations generated by my psychotherapists, in seated sessions obtained at a discount. For this reason, I have always had a profound empathy and pity for all who submit themselves to the imposition of having to belong to some sphere

The Illness

of existence on account of which they agree to demonstrate knowledge, force, or valor. To submit to an exam, a judgment, a contest, to any kind of jury, to be assessed by an equal so that they can pronounce a verdict and determine a grade, all such situations, unavoidable if one wishes to live in society, have always been humiliating and cruel predicaments for me, and I have persistently tried to avoid them, like one fleeing from evil.

Still, in order to make a living, and with acceptable criteria for "overcoming" difficulties, I have consented to enter into these extreme situations. For example, one of the challenges that produced the greatest suffering for me was accepting, in flagrant defiance of my terrible phobia, a teaching position at the University of Besançon, where, as I believe I mentioned before, my family and I spent a so-called first exile after the coup d'état of '66. There, while my psychosomatic manifestations found their way into my spinal column, a week after our arrival and after writing the letter to Queen Juliana's psychoanalyst, I had to begin teaching Latin American Literature and Civilization to a group of twenty-five students, people who were studying Spanish and who had their hopes set on an overseas position. My first class—and all others that followed, without exception—was committed in its entirety to sixty printed pages, at one read-aloud page per minute, to round out the hour required of me.

All that year, and those that followed, I spent sitting at the typewriter preparing the pages to be read in class. Even so, with all the security of having those pages on the desk in front of me, with everything foreseen, including possible answers to possible questions, every time I entered the classroom and the twenty-five hopeful overseas candidates rose and recited, *Bonjour, Madame,* I would experience that familiar hollow feeling in my stomach, or, more accurately, that hollowness would writhe and transform itself into a vacuum, so that from the very first evening, and, I might say, throughout my stay in France and at that university, that hollowness was there, as productive as the pages that were filled by its vacuum.

I do not know why I got myself into such threatening situations. I have to say that I felt an incredible relief at the end of each class, stepping out onto the street and into the plaza in front of the university with the sensation of having emerged victorious from a spectacular tournament. But the calm would last only a few hours, just long enough for me to catch my breath and become anxiety-stricken over the next class. From those years hundreds of pages survived narrating the history of Latin America, supposedly generating interest in the key texts of the literature of our countries and analyzing, with obsessive meticulousness, paragraph by paragraph, universe by universe, comma by comma, the works of Juan Rulfo. Later I disposed of those pages, one by one, or in sheaves of ten, in the incinerator of that Besançon house, before returning to Buenos Aires in 1970.

I believe that my examination phobia and the impossibility of overcoming it were precisely what prevented me from finishing my own studies. I never obtained a degree. I only needed to complete the last two courses but I could not, and those courses that I did manage to pass required extraordinary levels of concentration, accomplished through many late nights and early risings. I am convinced that my traumatized passage through the university, during which time I neither pursued nor gained a profession, left no traces in its wake; my colleagues and contemporaries, however, are all recognized professionals today in every corner of the world; many, almost all, held civilized jobs in the lands of their exile and have now returned to the country and occupy equally prestigious positions; they earned and are still earning honorable livings with their literary knowledge; they have found their niche. I have always told myself that I too could have reached such a position if I had only taken those last Ibero-American exams with Professor Verdugo, as the *usurper* of the Chair of Argentine Literature became known in 1966 after the previous occupant was fired.[1]

So, instead of dutifully finishing my studies and receiving a degree, knowing that without one a person can do nothing, neither teach, nor pursue a doctorate, nor participate in post-graduate seminars, nor obtain research grants, knowing that without a degree one is condemned to being a public servant or one more journalist among many, or a freelancer in assorted jobs, knowing that without a degree one is on the bottom rung and unable to ascend the ladder, one turns progressively into what is called a ghostwriter, in my case, a female ghostwriter, a profession for people without a college degree.

To be a ghostwriter, to remain hidden in the wings, behind the pages written by others, correcting, straightening out syntax, improving in the best of cases, and worsening in the worst of cases, texts that are to be signed by others, is a profession of faith and, over time, constitutes a neurosis of destiny. The mission of tutoring the sentences of others, of playing wet nurse over the verbal cradle of someone else's imagination, of another's unconscious mind, of being a municipal inspector of language and discourse, making incisions into paragraphs, isolating concepts with the insertion of relative pronouns, punctuating and adding

1. "Verdugo" means "executioner" in English.

quotation marks wherever possible and necessary, this mission was anathema to me and seemed impossible whenever I became conscious of what I was, in fact, doing; although I was articulate and wrote well—at least that is what people thought and that is why they paid me—all that I wrote for myself, for my own sake and benefit, became disjointed, and pieces of myself somehow found their ways into the writings of others, gestating and giving birth to unrecognizable monsters. Phrase by phrase, my phrase was dying, it dies, it was fading out, it fades out, it is correct, it is masked, it takes shape, it smiles, corrected.

I had to make it clear to that virtual psychiatrist that the condition of being second in all systems of classification, an award granted by fate, having been born between a brother and a sister, put me at the service, so to speak, of unscrupulous people who, while flattering me and thanking me profusely for what I had written beneath their signatures, would ultimately deny me; they denied me or depersonified me after having availed themselves of my abilities, of my trade they considered insignificant, that of putting ideas into writing. What is more, they often lacked ideas, and I had to invent writing to fill their empty structures or detour the text toward anecdotal questions in the absence of real concepts.

There are people who have extensive résumés, boasting articles and dense far-reaching essays that they never actually wrote, that were written for them by scribes like me. People who borrow or buy the words of others and then, puffed with pride, offer for their part a theoretical framework, without which, one might suppose, nothing would ever be understood, minimizing the importance of such secondary considerations as syntax. These people believe that not knowing how to write is an irrelevant disability, given that the only important thing is having and formulating a theory. In the empty framework in which these people vaingloriously revel, the craftsman or woman must toil on.

These imposters, who go about peddling their theoretical frameworks filled out by others, who always succeed in convincing institutions, foundations, national, international, and other academic agencies to acquire them, always have a whole gamut of ghostwriters behind them, and then there are those who will get hold of a linguist to tie their framework to a Saussurean system; or succeed in snaring a heavyweight philosopher to adapt it to a Foucaultian network; or seduce a feminist theoretician to spin out a proposal on the personal and the political, on equality and difference. These people have forged a personality by pitilessly taking transfusions of the competence of others.

The Cold That
Never Comes

My life in exile appears before me like a huge mural by Rivera, composed of protagonists and extras, leaders and buffoons, the living and the dead, the sick and the dispossessed, the corroded and the corrupted; the mural is the dense color of lead, with heavy and thick brushstrokes. There is anguish in the evocation, and, though I genuinely try to find some moment of collective happiness in the tableau (for there must have been some), a sense of melancholy predominates; nothing escapes the melancholy feeling of this gray, albeit intense, memory. This mural has a width and a height, a beginning and an end, and what stands out most in this delineated canvas, what undeniably vibrates in the landscape, is melancholia.

Nothing could be more anodyne and stupid than to say: "the exiles had it good"; this trivial remark, as a sort of excuse, is all too often passively accepted, like its counterpart of the same suit: "those who stayed in Argentina had it worse," and other simplistic variants that can only cause offense by comparing, as if it were a competition, situations that neither admit to, nor resist, placating classifications such as exile/interior exile, which are intended to differentiate and qualify the substance, the dough, so to speak, that has never been broken down or torn apart, never been truly explored, but has been maintained very neatly and compactly even though it embodies those destructive and devastating years from 1974 until the restoration of democracy, not to mention the aftereffects that even today evoke terror.

Time spent in exile has a trajectory like a great sweeping brushstroke, it has a broad open rhythm, its curves are like the ocean waves far from the coasts where there are no breakers and where they blend into the horizon; time takes place in the far beyond, in some other place, it is heard in the silence of the night, but it is brushed aside, one prefers not to perceive it because one assumes that the banishment will end, that it has all been some kind of parenthesis unrelated to the future.

Time is provisional, passing week by week on a train of successive stops; one reads the news, one considers events, one thinks in terms of options, in the imagination one confronts the adversary that has interfered with the passage of time, one imagines accumulating force with which to confront the superior enemy who occupies, also week by week and with constantly increasing firepower, the terrain that exiles have lost by being absent.

Discussions are endless, suspicions are endless; in the thickets and density of that timeless jungle there are no embankments to hold back the flow, the leaves do not fall, the cold does not come, the present never passes into the future. Events are illuminated as if in a theater, their significance exalted; paranoia has never had such a sibilant body as in this seasonless sojourn.

[19]

The Cold That Never Comes

One could not have imagined then that once the parenthesis had ended, if in fact it were ever going to end, what had ended would be perceived as a dense and variegated whole, as one single massive entity coursed through with multiple labyrinths whose cross sections would provoke such a gnawing sensation; the layers or strata thus exposed, in effect, rise up like ancient anthills, now abandoned, yet producing the same sensation of terror as if they were still teeming with life.

Terror is also provoked through evocation of the way in which seventy percent of our time was spent fretting over conditions in Argentina, that wretched country that had expelled us and of whose situation we never stopped talking—the sun never set, there were no new dawns—filling the cracks and hollows of our reality, so to speak, with Argentine substance, plugging all possible perforations with Argentine putty, stuffing the body and soul with that substance that produced neither pleasure nor fond memories, which only added a quota of death by entering or exiting our conscience (and still more while we slept, this quota entered our unconscious mind yielding immediate and magnified results, ever more powerful and horrible than while awake).

One almost always dreamed of death; one's dreams were constantly invaded by images of eviction and destitution; the sleeper would experience nights without end, naked, exposed, persecuted by invincible forces, tumbling into swirling torrents, missing one's train, leaving the house barefoot, losing one's documents, being driven in cars to unnamed destinations; a person lost stature, returned to an infancy immersed in clouds and layers of gauze, to rooms lit by distant ceiling lights and suddenly transformed into forests of shadows; people, in short, did not

have sweet dreams. And in one's waking hours the effect of these
dreams would recur like gusts of wind, interfering with any
form of transitory happiness.

Very naively, many exiles in Mexico continued to believe that, in
spite of everything, they were the world's best, and, thus, they
failed to mix into or merge with the population at large—their
neighbors, colleagues, or the like—but persisted in maintaining
very national traits and gestures that tended to provoke a kind of
vicarious shame felt by other exiles who, out of fear or timidity,
had opted to be as inconspicuous as possible. At government of-
fices, the immigration office, for example, they might speak ar-
rogantly or insistently, inciting a sudden obstinacy or defensive-
ness in response to their petulance by the Mexican official
attending them. The civil servant's expression would suddenly
change, as if drawing an internal curtain and at the same time
closing the gates leading either in or out; he or she would
neither listen nor respond to the arguments of the claimant; he
or she would withdraw into a shell, playing possum, which is a
common strategy, learned through the ages, among many species of animals in response to external threats.

This ability to play dead, which a fair number of psychoana-
lysts have adopted following Lacanian rules in an anecdotal and
reproductive fashion, is part of the Mexican culture and bureau-
cracy, almost part of its nature, and thus it is neither anecdotal
nor affected but, rather, inherent to the spirit. Confronted with
an arrogant Argentine, the Mexican's eyes go blind, the ears become deaf, and the lips are sealed, leading to a sense of absolute
impotence on the part of the claimant. It can take an Argentine

years to learn this method of distancing oneself from the exaggerations and vanities of one's fellows, and, if indeed the method is learned, it is not unlikely that it will carry with it a certain connotation of disdain, something that the Mexican avoids; taking the liberty to generalize, it seems to me that the Mexican puts into practice, perhaps unwittingly, a method for protecting one's mental health or one's proverbial dignity. In its extreme form, this weapon can be very effective and destructive; thus, there are many Argentines who, sure of themselves and their social position, have suffered this type of attack and have been overwhelmed by it, which logically engenders bitter commentaries against the aggressor, that is to say, their host.

Our bond to the country we were forced to leave conditioned our lives; there were even some who were never able to bear the sum of their losses, who passed their days remembering their old neighborhoods and idealizing customs that, one might wonder why, were considered paradigmatic of a lost paradise; that substance of Argentina that they missed seemed to be embedded in mythologies of little interest. Viewed today, both from near and afar—prior to the period of exile and after having returned to the country—that "iconography" and worshiping of objects that pervaded our fantasies, judged unemotionally, would seem insignificant, a patrimony with neither intellectual nor imaginary value.

There were affirmations of Argentine faith that were nothing but farces of patriotism, as, for example, the rapacity that could be produced by the Argentine flag as it hung from the wall together with the so-called Mexican "labarum patria" in the

The Cold That Never Comes

"house" of exile and that was twice brought forth with fervor and excitement, the first time being after the Argentine victory in the World Cup soccer championship, when an emotionally charged group paraded the flag through the streets of the city, raising their voices in victory chants; the other occasion was when this same group surrounded the British embassy, waving the flag, after the Argentine military regime waged a war, with which they identified, to recover the Falkland Islands.

Those longings for Argentine substance gave no respite; they adhered to one's body, suffused the mind, absorbed the bodily liquids, and left behind a desert wasteland; whoever could escape them, whoever could diminish their longings, did so with an iron will and determination to integrate themselves into their new environment. They had to learn a different way of life; that is, they had to learn to say hello to their neighbor, to yield the right-of-way, not to pass between two people who were engaged in conversation, not to pass plates in front of people at the table; to say *please* if they wanted something, and the corresponding conventions, *allow me* and *excuse me,* to express gratitude when necessary and even more than was necessary, responding to someone's *thank you* with *you're welcome*; not to interrupt people engaged in conversation, and when in control of the floor, to tone down as much as possible their verbal theatrics; to say *bless you* when someone sneezed, and *enjoy* when others started to eat; to offer one's own food to a recent arrival with a simple *care to join?* (practices that fell out of use long ago in Argentina by consensus of the haughty middle class); they had to learn to express hospitality with the courtesy form that con-

[23]

sisted of saying: *We'll be expecting you in your house,* which Mexicans used when inviting to their home an Argentine, who at first believed that the Mexicans were announcing a visit to the Argentine's home; the misunderstanding could go on for quite some time, repeating the phrase *your house,* or with the attempted clarification, *your own house,* with which phrase the Mexican wished to reaffirm the generous offer of his home to the foreigner; this generosity was never quite understood by the Argentine, whose interpretation was that the Mexican was assuming ownership of the Argentine's home, and the phrase *here you have your home* was never quite recognized, nor responded to with corresponding courtesy, which left the Argentine in poor standing and confirmed his inability to listen to others unlike himself.

These misunderstandings were like springboards that required the rapid and urgent learning of civility, and, after several years, it may be said with a degree of justice that some Argentines indeed learned to incorporate these laws of coexistence into their behavior and they could be seen in friendly get-togethers with Mexicans making special efforts to allow others to speak, yet with expressions on their faces of arduous restraint of their natural impulses to fill the silent spaces with the sound of their own voices and with an air of intense frustration at finding themselves obliged to give up the floor and employ more prudent tones.

At times they had to humbly eliminate certain linguistic forms from their own manner of speech, such as the use of *che* and the informal *vos* form of address; so, there they were, humbled even in the way they spoke the Spanish language, though it was almost impossible for them to completely erase their *por-*

The Cold That Never Comes

teño accent, that of Buenos Aires, for being so clearly distinctive. The humiliation included having to replace the rigorous Buenos Aires street-tough pronunciation of the *ye* with a kind of *iod,* which people from Córdoba and northward can do with such ease but which, on the lips of a *porteño,* causes extreme discomfort because it simply does not conform, and even when the speaker believes that he has it mastered, in no way does it resemble the Mexican *elle* and, even less, the *ye*; thus could be heard some very meager and starved *poios/pollos* (chickens) and *gainas/gallinas* (hens), hungry for a sense of belonging, which were like dropped stitches in the fabric of conversation.

It cannot be denied that the implantation of an Argentine in Mexico is indeed a rare historical phenomenon. And it continues to be a rather ridiculous spectacle, as seen over the years, as if through some secret vengeance Mexico was constantly resisting all attempts at appropriation by foreigners. The Argentines arrived and, with great care, erected their conglomerate living quarters, the so-called condominiums, where, for gregarious as well as financial reasons, they grouped together, accommodating themselves in Argentine style while, at the same time, declaring how much they loved Mexican arts and crafts. I always felt ashamed of myself, as I have said before, but particularly ashamed of others, every time I heard such phrases in the mouths of the recently arrived in Mexico, a kind of litany that deferred for a few moments the lament of the exile. I believe that, viewed from a distance, always from a distance, we knew very little about Mexican art and that the massive, if relative, acquisition of those cultural goods in the various markets was hardly governed by a criteria for quality. This may not sit well with those who read this, but there was incredible homogeneity in the furnishings of the houses of Argentines in Mexico; in almost every case, one encountered Taxco furniture or, more generally, rustic colonial-style furniture, acrylic tapestries with designs of Chiapaneca communities, serapes from Oaxaca, also synthetic, and the almost obsessive persistence with which they ate, at least in the early stages, from crockery containing lead; all of this created the sensation of being perpetually in the same house, whether one's own or someone else's, of always sitting in the same seats, drinking from the same blown-glass tumblers, seeing the same palm-leaf place mats and Michoacán tablecloths, and using the exact same leather seats, as if there were no differences in taste or intentions from one family to another and as if they all inhabited the same space.

These houses, in which a legitimate art object would only rarely appear, were very often transported to Argentina, exactly as they were, in enormous freight containers. This mark of uniformity, recognizable in many homes, has a melancholic effect because, although it may have been part of a defensive ideological unity while living in exile, in Argentina it serves no clear purpose but, rather, gives rise to nostalgia and longing, and one feels somewhat silly for believing that these small rituals of settling back onto Argentine soil will save one from the din of lost identity.

It makes me laugh now to see how we all arrange our temples, virtual Mexican altars to the dead, with offerings that include crocks without mole, fictional flour of nixtamal and chiles, and the perfunctory conversations about where one can get chiles or tomatillos strike me as pathetic with everyone saying that it is possible to find cilantro when everyone, yes everyone, knows that, in fact, cilantro makes Argentines sick, and the corn tortillas used to frustrate everyone because they preferred those made from wheat flour, and only very few Argentines ever really enjoyed eating frijoles; also, it truly upsets me to hear my compatriots, now called *Argenmex,* asking anyone who is traveling to bring back some chile chipotle because, for some unknown epicurean reason, it is the only kind they allow on their meat; it seems a great pity to me that their relation to chile is suddenly much greater than it ever was in situ and that they lost so many years during which they could have appreciated it and could have learned to discern between the *pasilla* and the *árbol,* the *morita* and the *mulato,* without abandoning their traditional hot ground pepper. I get impatient when I hear them say that it is possible to get chile serrano for sauces in Buenos Aires, when what Bolivian women sell in the market—seated on the ground like Mexican women, as is the manner of their race, and having a startling mirage effect on the *Argenmex*—is really chile árbol and cannot even remotely add the same flavor to a salsa verde; and it bores me to hear others and myself engaged in long dull conversations about Mexican eating habits with people who, I suspect, never ate anything other than breaded fried veal scaloppini and fried potatoes, and it seems incredible to me when they pronounce the letter *y* in the Mexican way while complaining of how much they miss the *papaya/papaia* from their table, a fruit whose memory they cherish but in fact rejected, and even more tedious do I find the fact that there is nothing with which we can diminish our nostalgia today, just as we could not diminish our nostalgia then with our *dulce de leche* and other ploys of outcasts.[1]

1. *Dulce de leche* is an Argentine caramel spread.

Poor Person's
Body

E very Sunday, returning to Mexico City, generally after
having spent the weekend in the house of friends, I
would write, without really writing it, the first paragraph of an extensive work that I always felt was a kind of "un-
shackling" experience, but very quickly the shackles would become entangled or simply break off. The initial sentence, to be
sure, would burst forth almost immediately, as soon as the auto-
mobile had covered the first few kilometers and we were leaving
the area of the volcanoes behind. The image that occurred to me
was this: *our progress leaves behind, in regular folds and at an impla-
cable rhythm, a trail that resembles memory, marked by posts, relays, sudden dark patches of dense tree groves, blind spots on the horizon, enormous pits of shadow, delicate glimmerings that seem to melt away the
burgeoning night and infuse it with light. Receding behind us, in the
measure that we continue our advance, there remains,* this is how I imagined it, *a gigantic sail, billowing in the wind (and sifted by time), a
screen through which the particles are strained and then disappear far
into the distance behind us.*

Poor Person's Body

These particles, I imagined, *were the dead who entered through my eyes and exited through the nape of my neck,* whirled through the mill of memory, left suspended in the road until the great sail would stir them up again with its passing. They would not plant themselves in my path or, for that matter, impose themselves on me; they were there as if waiting to be selected by my conscience with a certain legitimacy for appearing on that first page I was writing, there, in the backseat of a car. And what is stranger still in those figures suspended within my reach is that they did not presume to tell their grandiloquent stories but, rather, allowed me to feel, through their pure singularity, the gestures, words, and small parts they had played that meant something for me, their most representative actions, so to speak, that united them to me.

It was a vast cemetery, containing every type of death and dead; I made my choices in turns, and in the space of time that I retained one or another image, there stood isolated, in a prodigious synthesis, the particular quality for which each of these presences occupied a place in my life; a hand that I had once held in my own, an energy released from a body that had embraced me, an emotionally charged sigh that had left its mist upon my mirror. And behind me, through these kinds of images, life appeared perforated by thousands of losses, both great and small, and all escaped through tears in that great billowing sail.

In the act of remembering someone, one does not recover the whole person but, rather, some simple and apparently ephemeral modalities observed at some fleeting and seemingly insignificant moment. I would say that I am linked to the dead by these details that previously linked me to them in life as well:

through some quirk, through the expression of a desire in our domestic lives.

Mario Usabiaga became indelibly fixed in my memory one midday in the year 1981, when he impatiently scolded me for moving, by scarcely a few fractions of an inch, the steak that was cooking on the grill, and then, on that same occasion, he scolded me once more for salting the meat before turning it over; he explained that I had prevented *its being sealed* when I irresponsibly shifted it on the grill and that, by salting it before turning it over, I had caused it to lose its juices. Since that moment he has always been with me: every time I prepare a steak on the grill his two rules resonate and are repeated in my memory as if I were hearing them for the first time, and the image grew more intense after his death, that is, because he is dead. I do not know if, through this returning to that admonitory point of reference that binds me to him, I can find some kind of consolation, but one thing is certain: he will never leave me, and the day that his words no longer resound in my mind on those middays similar to the one on which he fixed his laws, I will have betrayed him in the annals of memory and, consequently, I will have been overcome by insignificance.

The most eloquent moments of that life, and the marks that they left in my memory, date back to 1970. The first scene is in Bahia Blanca; he is preparing an *asado,* a barbecue. His wife and children are there, and so are we. I do not notice then that he makes a point of not moving the meat, nor does he pierce it with a fork or salt the meat when turning it over but, rather, at the end. During the visit, without warning, Alberto Burnichón arrives, vital and nomadic editor, unique human being, who carries the poetry that he himself prints with the skill of a craftsman from city to city all over the country; a kind of father to all poets, kidnapped and killed by the military in 1976. Mario welcomes him as he would an ambassador, knowing well how to arouse Alberto's wisdom and sense of humor. In another scene, months later, Mario Usabiaga is dancing with Diana Galak after a dinner in my home; someone has put on music, and they rise as if in a dance hall, they embrace and move together gracefully, unaware of their audience or the space constricting their movements, among chairs in an area of no more than four floor tiles. He has separated from his wife and dances with this young woman who is so distant from the rest of us and so sure of her hold on him.

Some of his other gestures: the way he would throw back a switch of hair to keep it off his forehead as he bent over his typewriter during those interminable sessions of translating a book of more than a thousand pages from English to Spanish. Diana, the woman he was dancing with, was dying in the next room. And there is nothing more that can be said of that great tragic passage through life: abandonment, prison, abandonment, reconciliation, ultimate death. I have been searching for a letter of his, just last night I tore through all my belongings as if it were a matter of life and death; I got up in the middle of the night to sift through several folders, but it was not to be found, and, I thought, I must have put it in a special folder that I packed in the container and that was labeled RECORDATORIO, because it contained the last traces of my dead friends. While I was searching, I recalled a gesture of Mario Usabiaga, as if I were sculpting it myself, that I had denied myself for so long because it hurt me to recall his violent reaction, a physical stiffening as if confronting something too unbearable to face, which some of my verbal narratives—or the way in which I related them—had caused him. He could not tolerate my inability to express ideas in the way that he wanted, and once again I am seared by the sensation that I have disobeyed his laws, and the wound is reopened as I look for that letter in which, I am convinced, any rejection of me by him has disappeared, and his handwriting is free, elongated, as he says that he misses me, and it is excruciating when he describes his first months upon returning to Argentina, which were also to be the final ones of his life.

A life that is bound in every respect to what was said, done, or indicated by another person, a life that is bound to the commands of that other person each time one performs an action with repercussions in reality, a life such as this becomes something verging on the religious: one invokes, one quotes, one connects, one alludes to that other; one carries the weight of the world on one's shoulders, and if it is not Mario Usabiaga who appears in spirit to do so, then it will be another who takes the responsibility, with a similar stipulation: do not put the eggs in the pan while the oil is still cold, never; I like the toast more "browned"; one should not leave the tea leaves in the tea because it becomes toxic, and the same is true of *mate cocido*;[1] you have to "prick" the eggs before the water boils to prevent their cracking; and this absent person, animate or not, who once gave me these instructions, has unintentionally confined me within a closed system; he has bound me to reality, he binds me tooth and nail to reality's slightest projections, he condemns me to it without reprieve.

It would have been practically impossible for me to explain to that hypothetical analyst who sheltered me beneath his wing

1. *Mate cocido* is a popular Argentine green tea.

how these instructions regarding domestic habits kept me woven into reality, in control of my actions and with a hold over my psychic autonomy, such that I felt I was always being corrected, that is, always being set straight. And, then, I too exercised control over those around me, or over the ineptitudes of those around me, including my loved ones, a control that tended to become compulsive. These perfectionist obsessions that so impressed me in other people for a time became my own, as if having permitted others to correct me in turn gave me the munitions and prerogative to do the same to others.

It became intolerable for me during this period, and even now at times as if it were a conditioned reflex, to see someone cooking rice without taking extreme care, the mere idea that there should even exist people who, through improvisation or simple ineptitude, turn rice into mush; that they should not have reached a cultural stage that would allow them to grasp, if not the abstract concept, at least the aesthetic of loose, light grains of rice; I had become a veritable gendarme for the cooking of rice, and of pasta, and of potatoes, and I devoted myself to making people understand that the cooking process did not end the moment the cooking flames were extinguished, but that the food continued cooking beyond that moment, and that it was erroneous to conclude that a rice dish was properly cooked, just right, if one had not taken the precaution of turning off the flame a few minutes early, foreseeing the margin of time necessary to avoid producing mush.

The precise moment for rice, the precise moment for meat, all the precise moments for everything that, once missed, upset the balance of the universe, these were the moments of my obsession. And I had a very impatient and corrective attitude with anyone who infringed upon this harmony. This body of analysis, the obsession for minute detail, for its repetition, could have been taken as a symptom of self-censure manifested through its imposition on others, and because of others, thus having an even greater adverse and damaging effect on me. There was a subject of great volume and consistency to be observed, a mass of diverse fixations as well as phobias whose characteristic was to present itself in parts and counterparts, a dialectic that would be difficult to dissect.

If the "precise moments" were something like the closure of a shape or form, in a certain way a "wholeness" that was trespassed upon time and again by those who insisted on ignoring the limits, if people obstinately violated the correct states of the substances in question, it can clearly be seen that my obsession was to take note of what remained, what spilled over, and what, if allowed to pass certain limits, would ruin the food or spoil the optimum state of a process, with no possibility for recovery: what has passed beyond a certain limit can never return to its original condition. Never to reach completion, to always leave halfway through, to provide things with a margin for maturation, to be involved only in the initial stages of the evolution of an element and then to abandon it to its own inertia, to neither precipitate nor provide closure, these were the laws of my obsession that capped off my intentions and defined my desires.

But there was another obsession within the same body of analysis, correlative to the preceding, that was driven by lack. The inability to carry out activities to the point of completion was accompanied by a sensation of need, of exposure, of nakedness, and I use all three terms in succession because I believe they overlap. No one in any of the bogus therapies in which I was involved ever gave me a satisfactory explanation for my ambiguous relationship to clothing, probably the subject to which the terms need, exposure, and nudity most crudely apply. The nightmarish sensation of nudity was, for me, a constant in my waking hours. It is not an exaggeration to say that I find myself in a permanent state of clothing indigence; *I have nothing to wear* is accurate to summarize this condition. And to be in this condition, to have arrived at this point, is to be at the edge; beyond this point is the abyss.

I see myself searching through everything in my wardrobe; as a child, adolescent, and adult, I have always frantically searched my wardrobe for something to wear, whether jammed full or completely empty, because the besieged sensation I feel at these moments is independent of its contents. These grottos that suck me in have always spit me back out, naked, insecure, incomplete, and upset; whether awake or asleep I have never attained my dream of an outfit that would cover my nakedness and that would be reflected as "wholeness" in the mirror. Wardrobes have not been friendly to me in my life, and even today, about to reach the midcentury point, I cautiously avoid these yawning apertures and close them before going to sleep.

Like all mortals I have not been able to avoid the need for clothing, but I have never been able to carry out the act of dressing by myself. Through various ruses I have succeeded in getting people close to me, at all the different stages of my life, to dress me. It was a decision I made at a crucial moment, when, as a very young girl, by staying very still, as if made of porcelain, I persuaded a great-aunt to dress me from that day onward.

Poor Person's Body

This paralysis should not be taken as an easy solution; the game soon had dire consequences. Its most disturbing manifestation has been the physical dependency whose symptoms are most acute when I have to deal with the basic necessity of buying clothing. The terror begins as I enter a store, particularly one of those huge, massive department stores. Little by little, as the vast assortment is displayed before my eyes and passes through my hands, I begin to feel faint. My consciousness dissolves, disappears into folds of clothing, and I pass out.

Under these circumstances, mirrors contribute to unleash the crisis. The dressing room lights above the mirrors, my own inverted image, the way in which my body is covered by something strange, and the conviction that this foreign element is taking control of my body in that artificially illuminated small space, the whole experience, like in heartrending disaster novels, is a mortal blow. What is revealed in those secret sessions is not only craving, exposure, and nakedness but also the loathsome means of taking care of that basic necessity through the use of something borrowed, conceived somewhere for others, something that will satisfy neither the necessity nor me. I have often had this experience of falling unconscious while shopping and have thus inspired pity in those close to me who have regularly taken care of my needs without my even asking them, and in this way I have avoided entering stores or triptych-mirrored cubicles.

Clothing horrifies me, skirts bunch up, collars fail to cover the hairline at the nape of my neck; lapels fail to resolve the banality of clothing; there are no dresses for the ill-favored waistline; no footwear corrects bowlegs or knock-knees; no garment confers height or grace or frightens away nightmares; buying clothes is a miserable way to patch up one's life. Very rarely in my personal history have I ever felt what might be termed gratification from wearing a garment on my body, no one could ever convince me that something actually looked good hanging from my shoulders. Overwhelmed by this clothing trauma I have never wished to hear such compliments as, for example, that everything looks good on me, that all colors become me, or that there are no fashions that do not suit me to perfection; deaf to all comments intended to counter my terror of clothing, I consider all fashions to look ridiculous on my body, and it has been of no consolation to hear my friends telling me, when they gave me the clothes they no longer used, that I had a "poor person's body," meaning that everything suited me, flattered me, or became me, and to confirm this ductility I let them feel generous by departing from their houses loaded down with treasures that I carried home and were condemned to hang forever in my wardrobe. On the rare occasions when the taste of my benefactor coincided with my own, I would wear the clothes; I would surrender to the alienation of my body and soul precipitated by wearing someone else's clothes.

When I inherit, or keep as a souvenir, the clothing of a friend who has recently died, I dress myself *with them;* I have the feeling that I am wearing them, that I am sharing their shroud; however, I do not feel fear or apprehension but, rather, consolation, as if, by some sort of ingenious transmigration of the soul, they had left part of themselves in one of the sleeves, in the waistband, or in one of the cuffs. During my entire second pregnancy, more than twenty years ago, I wore a wool jacket that I inherited from a stranger, an Italian woman who had died and to whose house a friend took me in order to choose a few items of clothing. When

we arrived at that kinless woman's home, we found the wardrobe replete, although somewhat dreary, due to the circumstances; I chose the jacket I mentioned as well as a burgundy-
colored velvet blouse that had a border of painted gold flowers
on the fringes of the collar, sleeves, and hips. I never wore that
blouse but ended up giving it away as a gift without ever understanding why I took it in the first place, whether it was greed,
frivolity, or pity. What is certain is that I have felt guilty ever
since for having interrupted the eternal return of that woman
through me and that blouse, and, even now, twenty-five years
later, I remember the intense lavender fragrance that emanated
from her clothing and wardrobe; it is the overwhelming wave of
perfume that recalls this unknown woman to me.

The drawback of these pieces of clothing belonging to the
dead is that one hardly dares to discard or make gifts of them,
and so they eternally clutter the wardrobe. When one first
adopts these garments of absentee owners, one cannot fathom
the space that they will take up; they hang limply from their
perches, conforming to the shape of the hook or hanger, and,
eventually, become permanently misshapen; they cling to this
cold, dark life with the same stubbornness they previously held
to that other, perhaps warmer and more luminous, lifetime. I
still have a gray coat, on the end hanger in my Mexican wardrobe, that, without her knowing it, was left to me by my friend
Silvia Rudni, whose family let me have it as a keepsake; I wore it
often because it was a pleasure to wear Silvia on me, but suddenly, with the passage of time, pointy collars went out of fashion and, viewing us together in the mirror, I had a stroke of self-
pity: we were from the sixties living in the eighties.

Clothing begins to wear out of its own accord, the flanks

droop and disintegrate, exhausted; although this happens to everyone and everything in unequal measure, they all succumb over time. Few people perceive the fatigue of their fabrics because they usually abandon them before this occurs; it is a rare coat indeed that survives the social pressures that define it as being out of fashion, and it requires a strong ethic to accompany a coat through its fall from grace. I have lived my life dependent on my clothing, on the clothing of others that has become mine, the clothing of my dead friends, the clothing that others have given me through capricious benevolence or so as not to condemn it to oblivion; and this destiny, to go around wearing clothing at the tail end of its life cycle, to be one and the same as your clothing and at the same time to feel the horror of this relationship, is a misfortune whose significance is fair game for analysis.

When I was small, my family would dress me up in costumes for carnival, even forced me to do it against my wishes. I was made up as a "pickaninny," in the classic red dress with white polka dots, which also served as the costume for "the little traveling ant,"[2] skin covered with shoe polish and hair in small braids, insofar as my hair permitted, and finished off with red ribbons—for this is how little Negro girls, as well as ants, are presumed to appear—and also as a "gypsy," the headscarf adorned with a string of medals, hoops, ringlets dangling from the ears, and a long, full skirt with folds and pleats. When I became aware of how I disappeared beneath my costume or behind the coat of black salve applied to me, and that all that remained

---

2. *La hormiguita viajera* (The little traveling ant) is an Argentine children's story by Constancio C. Vigil.

of my identity were the whites of my eyes and the shine of my pupils, I would burst into tears and then be scolded for acting silly.

These costumes hang in my memory, but one in particular flutters in my mind like the shroud of the Grim Reaper, the wicked witch, or the "widow" of carnival, in the auditorium of my kindergarten, *The Perpetuo Socorro*. It was during the spring festivals, and they dressed me as a butterfly in a wispy dress of yellow gauze with coffee-colored stripes that outlined my insect shape and wings of wire covered with speckled tulle attached to my back. When we were just about to appear on stage to dance our number—flower girls and butterflies—with rigid antennae fixed to our hair, as well as the obligatory painted mole beside the mouth, Sister Serafina attempted at the last minute to secure my wings to my dress with a safety pin, but in her haste, the pin slipped and pierced my skin along with the material and tulle. I went out on stage as if run through by a dagger, and that pierced sensation has never left me. I have never told anyone about that incident, only Sor Serafina knew about it. From that day on I have never had any desire to go on stage again.

Curriculum
Vitae

After years spent in exile, if someone attributes the illnesses experienced upon returning to their country to the return itself, they will hear, in general, a whole series of soothing arguments. They will hear, for example, that the illness really has its own causes, that if someone returns and dies of a heart attack, or suffers a perforated ulcer, albeit without dying, or contracts chronic pharyngitis, any or all of these afflictions could have happened to the person anywhere, regardless of latitude or geography, and, moreover, the idea that these illnesses might be related to a lowering of bodily defenses, unilaterally declared by both body and soul upon setting foot on Argentine soil, is out of the question.

Anyone who speaks of a "universal" pathology, and rejects the idea of conditioning, ignores the fact that those who return inevitably practice casuistry and establish an entire doctrine simply by enumerating their ailments, deaths, and suicides, speaking only of what is most daunting and leaving aside other less evident deteriorations that, even if they occur in the most minimal degree, already constitute a form of illness. The way in which others, quite to the contrary, are disposed to meekly go along with the flow when they are included in the scheme of postexile destruction also fails to be convincing; submissive yet astute, they prefer to anticipate what lies ahead, thus practicing their own means of preempting misfortune. Rumination, adherence to common sense, exhibition of experience when it is supposed to have been objectified, all of these "positive" gestures are strategies for avoiding the spotlight and hiding in the shadows, in the opacity of denial. Nothing erases the facts, nothing obscures the edges of reality more than the classification of this selfsame reality.

To believe that one is in the know, to put on a show of skepticism in the face of all the good reasons for adapting oneself to one's country, produces nothing more than momentary relief and a fallacious sensation of control after which the letdown tends to be even more terrible. It is also illusory to take refuge in treatments, and, in truth, I do not feel that I escape these generalizations when I clamor for therapies and surreptitiously attempt to capture the attention of psychotherapists by slipping into the rootedness/uprootedness issue.

Among these attempts, there was one that was very peculiar. The psychoanalyst, no mere novice in these matters, preempted my appeal by offering me protection. He was a friend, so it was not surprising that he should call to ask how I was feeling and to find out how I was getting along in this business of returning to Argentina; he assumed that it had been difficult, that the plain and simple fact of always moving back and forth was costly; how much higher might be the cost of this return? he wondered, empathetic to my isolation. He was not going to let me down. At that time, unfortunately for me because I could have taken advantage of his willingness to protect me, I was actually feeling quite well, I was awakening to all kinds of stimuli, I was indulging in very elementary reactions, such as learning to appreciate the qualities of city lights or distinguishing street sounds, and, in particular, I was enchanted by the songs of birds native to my place of birth in Argentina; at that time, I did not know how to respond fairly to his concerns, within which I perceived an excessive zeal to help me avoid leaping headlong into the abyss.

I squandered all that he offered me and systematically failed in my responses to his expectations. *I should have been in a bad way* but, providentially, I was not, and thus I lost his interest, I let his kind gesture simply go to waste. He would have preferred my suffering, and I told myself, *I have to give him some justification for his concern, I have no right to sabotage this miracle,* and so, to make use of what he offered me, I shared with him some routine misgivings, but this did not satisfy him. I recalled numerous events that had united us in the past and that had slipped his memory. He felt terrible; forgotten episodes rose to the surface of his life and permeated his nights; he neglected his patients, becoming one himself as a result of some deep unhappiness I had stirred up, and he finally ran away.

One night, months after so irresponsibly wasting that opportunity and unable to make amends, I became aware of my isolation. Now my anguish indeed cried out for an attentive ear, and I regretted having let myself be distracted by the birdsongs and other such foolishness. I had no recourse other than to turn to an old friend, now famous for having set up a therapeutic practice combining Freudian psychoanalysis, Zen Buddhism, and the way of the Tao, and whose success is derived from *making one think.*

Curriculum Vitae

As I was going to the appointment in which she planned to awaken this repressed faculty of *thought* in me, with the added ingredient of *helping one to change*—"think in order to change" —I had an almost demented faith in her gifts, whether physical, mental, exorcistic, or oracular. At the time, I was in such bad shape that, as a precaution, I avoided stepping out on my ninth-floor balcony. Just listening to her was enough to have the immediate sensation that she was applying a lukewarm compress to my very being, that she was lathering me with her sugary sweet breath; she had a tender gaze that was, quite frankly, unbearable, and her oozing vapors were a sign not of weakness but, rather, of her professed power to understand me.

There was no magical sleight of hand: like someone organizing classified ads clipped from the newspaper, she began to organize a list of employment "opportunities" for me, but not without first asking, in a mysterious and conspiratorial tone, as if trying to get me to reveal some kind of secret vice, *what did I really want to do in Argentina, what was it that most interested me, what troubled me, what excited me, but truly,* she said, *what is it that you want to do,* posing the question in such a way that there could be no doubt of her seriousness. I did not answer at first, perhaps as a defense against the onslaught, but after a few minutes, beneath her inquisitive and "profound" gaze, I foolishly began to enumerate my professional merits, including my activities during my years in exile, which she had no reason to know anything about, as if I were reading her my curriculum vitae, and the sum of interests that had at one time or another attracted me was so profuse and delirious that, little by little, my answer seemed to completely swerve off course. Unstoppable, it could only culminate in a misunderstanding.

Curriculum Vitae

Making an effort, and only after looking deeply into my soul as if saying confession, I said that *fundamentally* what interested me was *writing,* feeling miserably unhappy, wanting to slink away as soon as possible, on the verge of tears, but out of politeness remaining a while longer with my inquisitive-eyed friend, who went on reading me my possibilities, wholly nonplussed by my expressed main interest; in truth, she had immediately changed the subject, as if rather than *to write,* I had said *to die* or *to kill.* My erstwhile therapist really took the cake.

I wanted nothing else: *to write,* I said with the inflection of one who is making an apology; *to write,* I said in a whisper, and this seemed to give her a start; and, truly, the decision to write in no way resembles a decision related to gainful employment, but she wanted to nudge me toward something more pragmatic, mentioning people who prepared texts for advertising campaigns or art promoters who worked for art dealers. I did not understand. How was it possible that in response to confessing my desire to write she should make such wild hypotheses regarding my person? We finished our second cups of coffee, and she continued confronting me with these practical suggestions of her own contrivance, which especially, and among others, consisted in a phenomenal apparatus for, according to her objectives, *providing support and stimulus and practical attainment* of the most personal and buried desires of her client-patients.

I could already see the cataclysm coming. I was going to tell her, once and for all, that until that moment I had never realized the extent to which two people could speak in, and from, such different perspectives without disqualifying one or praising the other; calmly, I was going to tell her that we were speaking on two different levels and that, perhaps, she, with all of her advice, believed in good faith that those two levels had some point in common but, in fact—and I really did not want to disappoint her—strictly speaking, I was not looking for work; I was going to tell her all of this, but I wisely held back, thus avoiding that almost inevitable statement in such conversations when my listener grows weary of my resistance to the solutions they are offering: "Alright, then, what is it that you want?" which would have meant the end to our conversation. I said nothing, I swallowed hard and went on chattering in that echoless chamber. What is certain is that she pushed me to my limits; her complacent idea of the world made me wish, intensely, to not be there, to be able to erase through some kind of magic everything that had transpired across that table, everything we had said; I could not take any more of her good intentions toward the lost souls of the night, the blind in the roadways, of showing them the supposed light that would guide them to their own truths and, in a mechanical relation of cause and effect, to the springboard of a well-paid position of employment that would return these outcasts of the world to a position in the world. The night ended in dry heaves that led, after I had finally returned home and forever taken leave of my friend, to an attack of gastritis, as was to be expected.

Oracles

I have already mentioned that my first exile lasted until the end of 1970, following the coup of 1966; my second exile was from 1974 to 1986, which made for a total of sixteen years living outside the country due to coups, dictatorships, and complicit civil-military regimes. Not a low count by any measure, even when compared with the Spanish exile experience. All in all, the years added up: I have to admit, however, that of those sixteen years, three can be discounted because we could have returned to Argentina sooner, immediately following the end of the Falkland Islands war, as many people did, or in the wake of the elections and the restoration of democracy, as did many more, but, in any case, those years, for a person of any age, were very significant. I left the country, for example, in my "first exile," just before my twenty-seventh birthday; I returned just before turning thirty-one; I left again at thirty-four and returned a woman of forty-seven; the periods flew by, tornado-like, leaving me in sudden states of confusion concerning the passage of time. During the insanity, it was not unusual for the hemispheres to seem to merge or for the cardinal points to get lost or distorted. The East shifted over toward the West, the South toward the North, and vice versa, and I could not shrug this sensation off merely by reasoning that it all depended on where one stood at any given moment.

This tenuous perspective persisted in the Valley of Mexico and was all the more conspicuous due to the lack of definite seasons, so distinct in other latitudes. Despite the lack of a clearly defined autumn, or an unequivocal winter, winter was still obstinately present via the fashions offered in the marketplace, just as the spring, summer, and fall collections also appeared in their turns, no matter that when it rained in summer it was colder than in winter and that a midday in winter tended to be, quite frankly, tropical, transporting a person through various seasons all in the same day.

The years ceased to roll along during that long parenthesis. Perhaps this dislocation was a consequence, or a parallel symptom, of a destructuralization of exile itself, but no one ventured to analyze such questions, nor did anyone attempt to set their "biological clock-in-exile." I brought the subject up with my psychologist, the one who treated me when my throat was attacked by golden blisters; I told him I was upset about missing my birthdays, that I had this crazy idea that time was standing still, and that, inasmuch as the present seemed to be frozen, the future had become vast and infinite; I was acutely aware that this illusion was really a kind of suspended state portending that at any given moment we would have to begin a countdown from a starting point whose outcome was wholly unpredictable.

Sure enough, ten years after that rather imprecise premonition, on my first trip back to Buenos Aires, all in a flash, the years crashed down on me, and the assault was so brutal that I found myself gasping for breath. I had always thought that the inclusion in certain literary works written by women of a scene in which a woman stands before a mirror and suddenly sees herself clearly, confirming the ravages of time upon her face and then plunging into deep depression, was one that could let the air out of any piece of writing, and I swore to avoid it in my own writing. Every time I read, "She saw herself in the mirror," with all the inevitable trappings, the attendant sentiments and ideologies, I stopped reading. And thus forewarned, nonetheless, on my first trip to Buenos Aires in 1984, purely out of curiosity and highly charged with negativity, I found myself examining my own face in the mirror and discovering, all in an instant, in my skin, my eyes, the corners of my mouth, the cyclone of those ten years; and it was not the discovery of wrinkles, or other signs of decrepitude; it was something else, a fine gray powder, rather macabre, like a patina, that covered the totality of my being. My image had acquired the sepia tone of old photographs, an ashen glow. I would say that, until that revealing moment, I shared the view and the sensation that the people of Argentina had aged very much while those of us who had left, in contrast, had remained the same, suspended in that parenthesis of impotence; I see now that those compatriots who lived outside the country, two or three years after having returned, show the passage of time like any other mortal and that they show it even more than those of the same generation who remained, as if the illusion of that fantastic interim had charged us double the going price and we had been condemned to even greater bodily deterioration. Thus was I reflected in the mirror: a fan long kept closed that, little by little, as it was allowed to unfold, produced a multiplier effect upon the years.

Oracles

With the fan laid open and conscious of spatiotemporal falli-
bility, it was too late for me to turn back; if one senses the limit,
if one reaches the frontiers of physical and moral resistance, and
if this condition reaches its point of greatest intensity—if it is
revived, in a word—in one's own country and after so many
years of absence, then, I reasoned, one cannot dodge the question, and, as if my reasoning could assume a physical manifestation in order to operate under the circumstances, I imagined an
ascending line, one that curved upward and circled back on itself and then rose again. This line that lifted me up and whipped
me along my trajectory was the idea in motion that served to
explain my return. And only by complying with this parabolic
idea would it be possible for me to go on living. This image also
worked as a kind of incantation: to return, the recurring act
whose promise of repetition did not seem at all strange to me
given that there had been no passage of time during my Mexican
parenthesis, it was going to be like the kiss of the prince that
awoke the sleeping beauty.

The first time I returned to Argentina was in 1984. My most
fervent desire was that the plane should pass beyond its destination, that it should miss the Ezeiza airport; then I thought that
this missed destination would mean never again setting foot on
Argentine soil, nor on any other soil. I did not think then of Cindal, that remote death, overwhelmed as I was by the abundance
of dozens of other more recent deaths that had much more reason to occupy my thoughts for having been, in many cases, so
close to me personally. There was a justification in wishing the
plane to fly off course and into oblivion. After ten years of absence, I stayed for just one month. During the first few days I
could not even set foot in the street; I stayed closeted in the

space of the room where I slept, and it would have been impossible for me to overcome my agoraphobia had it not been for the friend who was putting me up, who took me by the hand one day and urged me to go out.

On that first outing, we walked along Vicente López Street in the direction of Junín Street. We passed in front of the municipal marketplace, the one that formerly spilled out onto the street, with stalls placed along the walls of the Recoleta cemetery, just a few feet from the café, La Biela, and we observed how smug and resplendent the rubber trees were in the park, and I remembered the time I had seen a man, a homeless man, but not like Calvino's Baron in the trees, asleep on the thickest branch of one of the oldest trees; a few feet away from that tree, whose foliaged image was still trapped in my memory, observing the many people now seated below contentedly sipping their coffees or teas in the shade of that same tree, I could not control the spasms of gastritis—classified as "emotional" according to the diagnosis of 1981—and without uttering a word, because I had lost the reflex of asking for help, or admitting that behind my lips there rose a flood of saliva, I retained absolute control over my senses and feelings and swallowed a nausea that any other person with less control would have unleashed with a shriek of pain, opting for the spontaneous and genuine relief of nausea that is plainly and simply to vomit. I scarcely said a word other than that I felt a slight spell of dizziness and sat down in a doorway to regain my composure. From that moment on, I only went out of the house for purposes of reconnaissance: the street where I used to live, the street where they killed "Fulano," the street where I last saw "Mengano," the plaza where they kidnapped "Perengano"; Fulano, Mengano, and Perengano, poor nominal substitutes in the Spanish language to avoid naming or connoting a person, and that, by not naming, merely enumerate.

". . . but the weather turned around . . ." was the idea etched in the minds of those of us who read Dylan Thomas at the end of the fifties and the beginning of the sixties; to surrender myself to this idea was in a certain way to save myself, as if some kind of mystical invocation could extract me from my stagnation and bring about change. Throughout my years of exile I had been reading, on a daily basis, the *I Ching*, the book of changes, book-guide-priest-analyst, whose therapeutic benefits I received in the mornings and, in times of extreme crisis, twice daily, morning and night.

Wrapped in the hide of a yellow cow was the phrase that came up when I threw three dragons with the coins (in Mexico, the dragons are eagles and on the reverse side of the coin are suns); the hexagram was *Ko* (Revolution) and the line said: *Changes should be made only when there is no other option. For this reason, extreme restraint is necessary from the start. One must affirm oneself, exercise self-control.* In the dialectic of change, the color yellow is the happy medium, and the cow is the symbol of docility. The hexagram, upon reading the oracle when it was past time for me to make a decision regarding my return, only produced uncertainty. It told me quite clearly that, for the moment, I should *abstain from doing anything, inasmuch as all premature actions bring misfortune.* I have always admired the warrior metaphors in the "guide-book," that logic of confrontation that describes the structure of human relations. I was accustomed to abiding by the chance indications of the hexagram in my daily activities, but after that first reading, before deciding to change, I realized that the war was going to be intense. The Chinese character *Ko* signifies, in its original meaning, *the skin of an animal that, over the course of time, changes its skin by shedding.*

The signs were plentiful. A few months later, *Ko* appeared for me again, and I drew a nine—three dragons—which signified: *The great man changes like a tiger: the skin of a tiger, with clearly visible black stripes on a yellow background, has a distinctive appearance from a distance. The same occurs in a revolution incited by a great man: the lines are large and clear, visible and comprehensible to anyone.* And, dispensing with all hesitation, the line told me: *For this reason, you should not consult your oracle first, inasmuch as you have the spontaneous support of your people.*

In philosophical terms, although the politics of power and the sphere of the individual form a single unit, according to the book of changes, it is important to know how to distinguish between the two; but this time the hexagram appeared with a univocal message: revolution was everything, for both the individual and the people. A note at the foot of the page was still more exhilarating. It said: *Cf. Goethe's story, "Das Märchen," in which the phrase "The time is at hand!" is repeated three times before the great transformation begins.*

I take up three coins, their faces now show the value of five cents on one side, and Argentine pumas appear on the other— the eagle and sun, flight and brilliance, are far from me now—I concentrate on my four returns to Argentina, the first for one month in 1984, the second for two months in 1986, the third for eight months in 1987, and the fourth, which begins with the toss of these coins; I do not formulate any particular question for the oracle, just a vague and general query concerning the new stage I am about to begin. The first toss, first line, a dragon (puma); the second, two pumas; the third, same as the preceding; the fourth, one puma; the fifth, two pumas; the sixth, two pumas; I notice that the lines of the two trigrams, upper and lower, are all equal, none are variable, and, thus, they do not form a second hexagram. There is no future, or the oracle says nothing beyond the present line; the present bears the entire burden, it would seem to have always been the "now" of this everlasting day. The hexagram is *chen*, which arouses (shock, thunder): it represents the elder son, he who follows the rules with energy and potency. One line of yang grows below two lines of ying and makes its way upward. This movement is so violent that it awakens terror. It is symbolized by the thunder that arises from the earth and, with the shock, causes fear and trembling.

The shock that sows fear for a hundred miles all around nonetheless does not topple *the sacrificial spoon and chalice*. So often, the echo has filled my ears; for the book, it is the manifestation of God in the depths of the earth, and, as the sound of God, it wreaks fear in men. The book gives me another opportunity, its dialectic of weights and counterweights tells me that this time the fear of God is good because it will be followed by joy and contentment. And it adds: *When a man has learned in his heart the meaning of fear and trembling, he will be safe from all panic caused by external influences.* Let the thunder resound and disseminate terror for a hundred miles around: man will go on being modest and reverent in spirit, and he will not interrupt the ritual of sacrifice; for this reason, neither the spoon nor the chalice will fall.

The Order
of the Day

No oracle foretells what will happen better than the very decision to make things happen. Predicting outcomes also constitutes a sort of neurosis of destiny; during all the years in which time seemed to stand still, it was necessary to cling to facts and, most importantly, not to miss a single curve in one's path or to overlook the milestones. Given that we were excluded from what was happening in Argentina, given that it was others who buried the dead, others who ate at our tables and slept in our beds, others who continued belonging to that place and to that present, and given that we could not return and that no one was pleading on our behalf or demanding that we return, we lived by proxy, through third parties, struggling with the memory of a country that was thousands of kilometers away and transporting it to the barrios of Aguilas and Tlacopac, to the streets of Calzada del Desierto de los Leones and Callejón de la Rosa, the neighborhoods and streets, respectively, of our two successive headquarters.

There, during many, many nights, deranged Argentines would come together: with statutes, petitions by the majority and the minority, orders of the day, records of proceedings, organizational diagrams, requests for information, elections. If one figures that some ten hours per week were devoted to those meetings, that is, forty hours each month, or four hundred and eighty hours annually, it can be supposed that after ten years of exile, we spent some five thousand hours in meetings, and this figure, of course, should be doubled because the meetings were always much longer than any mere average; to discuss, dissent, suspect was our way of constructing a country out of that Argentine limbo that was our exile, and our mission did not admit temporal limits. In fact, the figure should be quadrupled because there were other subgroups in other "houses," and there, also, the legalistic discussions were undoubtedly interminable.

The verbal constructions were numerous and varied, what was said during those meetings lasting far into the morning hours, whatever the position being defended, took the form of a terraced pyramid with thousands of lines of reasoning striving toward the topmost plateau, the truest, the one that would finally sustain an effective proposal; our hearts were aflame but the underlying spirit was, in principle, to reach agreement. It did not take long for this fallacious unity to fall apart. In truth, no iron will could have prevented the proliferation of these divisions, and the fact that those differences only multiplied revealed the natural impossibility of consensus, fueling still more discrepancies and alliances, which was a minimum requirement for occupying our time spent in political exile.

Those positions, all expressed in a single space, at times convinced me to take sides. I rejected any hint at a populist appeal, I detested the ponderous and elegant tone of the "illustrious" discourse, but I was nonetheless attracted to the terraced lines of reasoning, each true to its own style, as if casting a rope to the listener and letting him rise, knot by knot, to the summit of the argument, sparing neither vertigo nor suspense. Of this type of discourse there were few exponents. In principle, the style consists in establishing a pact with one's interlocutor based on a shared suspicion, not the suspicion of a particular person or occurrence but, rather, understood as an "epistemological" attitude: one's view of reality is based on an analysis that one is initially invited to share, because at some prior moment whoever is leading the analysis or evaluation has already gained the listener's confidence; whoever constructs the discourse on the subject in question counts upon our mutual suspicions and proposes an interplay of suppositions that are imperceptible to the dimwitted; our only possibility of following along is to grasp onto the rope that has been dangled before us; we are not given crutches, but, rather, we are urged to rise up defiantly, without revealing our doubts or hesitation. Entering this discipline implies running certain serious psychological risks because if, in the course of the exercise, one misses a step or dares to question a weak point, the tension of the whole construction may slacken and jeopardize the entire communication. There were clever arguments for not exposing the weak link: to postpone, for example, the questioning of the vague point and to wait patiently for its clarification; to trust in the general line of reasoning and relieve the pressure on the intervening points; to make, in the end, an effort to value one's own personal judgment comparable in magnitude to the distinction conferred by the person who had selected us as audience for his or her thoughts.

It was difficult, in exile, to sustain these methods of reflection that avoided direct communication and, rather, forced one to think. Alone and against the current, those who tried found that they were often regarded as party poopers, perhaps because they relentlessly pursued the fundamental questions: the nature of the "enemy" and one's position in relation to him—dominated, confined, trapped between the antipodes, at a crossroads, caught in duplicity, in two-facedness and perverse infiltrations. This type of intelligence could detect, in the intelligence of others, the point at which some kind of transaction was taking place. It was a structural paranoia that, in the end, once set in motion, could not be stopped.

There were other models for expression and thought, but our state of alertness and pessimism enabled us to detect the dangers, like pitfalls, that were misleading and had to be avoided: dubious self-criticism, for instance, whereby the subject, in order to accomplish his or her purpose, crossed to the other side of the river, in a sort of detachment from one's own identity, leaving in identity's place those responsible for the political or strategic errors that were now being questioned and that up until that very moment were one's own spitting image, without letting the listener become aware of the origin and trajectory of the switch; hypercriticism of the efforts of others, always considering the modest projects presented to them as "not political enough"; discouraged, the hypercritics would regain their positive self-images by no longer attending the meetings, rescuing themselves from the drawn-out sessions that lasted until daybreak; there were zealous ways of thinking that focused on such extreme terms as *annihilation* and *genocide,* among others, for describing the military repression and the disadvantages they represented, eliminating these terms from their denunciations, thus fertilizing, already in the seventies, the bicephalous idea of the two demons.

I could not establish what the effects were of that prolonged activity into which we invested so much passion; I do not know what the consequences of all that work might have been, nor do I know by which means, little by little, the work disappeared—completely and utterly disappeared—during the period of social and political reconstruction after the return of democracy. And I wonder, where is the energy of that powerful libido that drove us all to sit around a table for hours and hours, chain-smoking and ingesting liters of coffee, and where, for example, is the distrust that was aroused in me, more pleasant than bitter, in the face of what I perceived to be defections, which turned everything into that emotional torrent that infused my life with both hatred and love, what happened to the differences or the coincidences, where are the people whose judgments caused us to consider and reflect, what happened to the concern for the shady deals, the reconciliations, and the ruptures that Miguel Angel Piccato, who died in exile, used to write about in the weekly dispatches he would send me? That political cathedral, without territorial foundations, erected in Mexico during whole days and nights of forced labor, now lies in ruins, the practices carried out there absorbed by a thick and pachyder-mous skin. And the topological intelligence that distributed facts and circumstances, that grasped the inflections of discourses and discerned the pulse and tension of the attacks against the dictatorship, no longer discovers an opening into which to insert itself and gain leverage; enfeebled, it withdraws.

Emissary

"I don't think I could bear, either physically or mentally, the return to Asturias. In the world of memories, Asturias will always be a kind of mythical land for me. You've been there . . . The entrance through the doorway of Pajares is unreal, almost subrealistic [*sic*]. One doesn't enter Asturias, one descends into Asturias. The first thing one encounters are the clouds, which are not overhead but, rather, underfoot . . . You have to pass through the clouds in order to find the valleys and the mountains. It's all unreal, and that's how it remains in my memory," so spoke Ovidio Gondi.

A republican and a socialist, he arrived in Mexico during the exile of '39, when he was twenty-seven years old, and he never planned to return to Spain; he could not bring himself to return when given the opportunity, after the death of Franco, and he no longer wished to. He was the assistant director of a weekly, founded in the forties, for which he had worked ever since, on the first floor of an old house in Colonia Roma, writing almost the entire magazine, but particularly a section called "American Continent," or "America, from Pole to Pole," I no longer remember; I was put in charge of "The Other Continents," which, by process of elimination, included Asia, Africa, and Europe, a total of eighty manuscript pages, twenty-eight lines each, sixty-five spaces per line, every week, which Gondi approved or disapproved of according to the most rigorous literary and journalistic criteria. I inherited the position from Andrés Soliz Rada, a Bolivian exile who, following the military coup of '71 that deposed General Torres, first lived in Argentina and then in Mexico; after the famous hunger strike of '78, which marked the beginning of the end for the military dictatorship in Bolivia, Soliz decided to return to his country. Before leaving, he called me and said, confidentially, "You've got to take advantage of this breach in the trenches," and he introduced me to Ovidio Gondi.

Whether to be in my country or outside of it, whether to lose it or recover it, that was my obsession, and it was such a strong and pervasive obsession that I decided I had to exercise some influence over it, to reorient it in some way, or at least to relate it to that of other exiles, my peers, who were living at the time, in 1979, in Europe, and so I decided to go and see them. It has been eight years since that bold enterprise, and I cannot seem to recall the reservations with which I set out on that pilgrimage in search of other exiles, battered people who had lost children, who had been widowed, or who had fortuitously survived massacres. It was not a return but, rather, a way of defining imaginary territory, not to lose it, not to permit one's senses to be beaten down. I also set out to visit Asturias, Gondi's village, to return in his place and later report to him all that I had seen; even knowing that my voyage would not modify his intentions, I believed that I could restore to him something of his past.

Very late one night or early in the morning, coming from Madrid, I reached the clouds of Asturias; we passed through Campomanes, La Cobertoria, Ujo, Santullano, Mieres, Ablaña, Olloniego, until the clouds suddenly seemed to spread out at our feet and the wheels of the train sent them rolling in great waves toward the mountain slopes. From the white compartment of the train, isolated from the night as if in a hermetic capsule, I observed the beginnings of the mists that continued thereafter, unabated, after we had left the Castilian plains behind. There, peering into the night through my window, I had no doubts about the restorative logic of my mission; nevertheless I grew increasingly restless and was no longer sure that I could resist the onslaught of melancholia. It occurred to me that far away, that same day and the next, and all the days that would follow for the next two months of my absence, Ovidio Gondi would be imagining my arrival in Oviedo, at the doors of heaven and, moreover, the moment in which I would stand at the doors of Sama de Langreo, inhaling the clean and humid air, vanquishing the inevitable sensations of alienation. I knew that he was thinking of me, entrusted as I was with an obligation and bound by a promise through whose fulfillment the fantasy of returning would be both expressed and extinguished in a simultaneous interplay of delegations, me for him, him for me, without end. He, in Mexico, perhaps feared that I might back down at the last moment, but, at the same time, he must have hoped that the undertaking would be frustrated on its own because, in fact, to send an emissary was really the beginning of a reconciliation, it was to border on affection, even embrace it, and he had resolved never to return to Spain. Together we had devised the plan. In Oviedo, I would try to find don Manuel Ordax, his only remaining friend; he would guide me to Sama de Langreo, where the

Emissary

Gondi family lived during the civil war, and from there we would go to El Entrego, Gondi's place of birth.

Don Manuel Ordax performed the Celtic rituals. He told me: "Here, we used to drink cider," and he poured some cider onto the sawdust floor of the cantina; "Here was the village meeting house, the Casa del Pueblo, which has now been reopened"; "Here, in this plaza, we used to play"; "Here, Ovidio read me a poem about boats"; "Tell him that we were in front of his parents' house." In this way we advanced through the streets, turning corners, and he indicated, pointed out, oriented successive perspectives, directing me toward the general or the specific, the large and the small, and I, the privileged witness, stored in my memory my own reckoning of all that I saw, I gathered for Gondi my impressions, the scorching heat suspended over the treetops in the plaza, over the low housetops in Sama, and also paralyzing the old men sitting on benches, a "projection" of Gondi himself had there never been a war, had his people not been lined up and shot, had he not fled into exile, a projection in which he appeared beside those memory-ridden old men, retired and humble. And thus his negation was justified, his refusal to return.

Ordax did not waste an instant: he stopped the eldest among them right there on the street and asked: "Did you know Ovidio González Díaz, known as Gondi for short?" And the people stared at him, stupefied, and even more stupefied when he offered a wealth of details describing the Gondi family. Until, finally, he awakened someone's recollection, a señora, an elderly woman of some seventy years of age, rigorously dressed in mourning, who said "yes," how could she not have known them; after all, she was Manolita, the widow of Pepín Carrocera, shot

[63]

when he was twenty-nine years old in '38, she knew don Perfecto González very well, Ovidio's father, "they shot him three years after the war ended, just imagine!" and she took us a few paces down the street and into her house, flustered by the rush of recollections we had dislodged in her memory. And she seized upon one memory, while releasing another, by threes and fours she spread them out like fans, gathering them together, stacking them like cards; such occasions do not occur often in the life of a widow, left all alone at the end of a lifetime spent raising children.

Suddenly she produces some photos from a large black change purse, the same one that she was carrying on her errands when we approached her. One, taken by a Reflex camera, is very worn with tattered edges; it shows an empty field, with an unfinished wall in the background; in another, in color, the wall has been completed, and there is a cross, like a monument with no name written on it, just the word PAX. "In this field they shot them. They took my man together with thirty-five others, in the boats, on the twenty-fourth of June," the widow says. "The monument was put there by Franco himself during the fifties."

"So that you can tell Gondi"—the leitmotif never ceases, it fills all the voids left by emotion and goodwill; the war goes on, nothing ends, he does not return, but I have become the emissary, and, without even noticing it at the time, when the train leaves the clouds and begins its descent toward Madrid, I begin my own premature return to Argentina, there, in Spain itself. "Everything is unreal, and that's how it remains in one's memory," Ovidio Gondi insists.

Cellular
Chambers

weird

The alignment of identical openings the length, breadth, and depth of a surface with the soft, morbid consistency of brimming honeycomb, even one that is devoid of harvest, would produce in me what I came to call the *cellular effect*: the sudden irrepressible biological need to bite into something. Not to bite with my teeth, mind you, but with some other, more general human device not situated in the body but, rather, in the vague spaces of the so-called mind. My teeth, in truth, would not bristle, nor would they tremble, as if set on edge, but something in my mouth would nevertheless shift and soften, including my teeth, whenever I had this sudden urge and resulting need to penetrate or fuse with the cellular surface.

The-night-has-a-thousand-eyes could drive me mad: the vast perforated surface, a sponge whose pores absorb human understanding. It was not necessary for the structure of cellular blocks to be particularly extensive; it might take the form of narrow chains, or lines of paired cells, or branches of no more than a few. On the lavender flower, for example, the calyxes are distributed along the stem; if one holds the stem horizontally between one's fingers, with the tip pointing either to the left or to the right, in profile, the sensation begins to impose itself because the formation consists of <u>cerulean</u>-blue grains and they are jolting to the sense of touch; one rotates the stem ever so slightly, raising it up to eye level; the small black mouths of the <u>corolla</u> cluster together, like miniature raised cannons, and one has the <u>tubuliflorous</u> urge to bite, irrepressible and incomprehensible, and one is wracked by internal chills and spasms.

There are fungi that, when nascent [born], are convex but that hollow out like funnels as they grow; mushrooms that mature in clusters and bunches, with nipples at their centers when young (cf. José Juan Tablada), emitting phosphorescent lights through the night, like "fireballs"; mushrooms with conical skullcaps, or like church bells, fragile, with long hollow stems; trembling mushrooms with cat's tongue surfaces; mushrooms whose cells are laminae, flakes, small nests, or craters; furrowed, fringed, coral-shaped, sporadic mushrooms; mushrooms, when caught in my sight, at my feet or at eye level, would unleash that familiar sense of desperation whose indefinite origin would drive me away from wherever I was with all possible haste.

At the height of my sensitivity to this effect, all of reality appeared to be distributed in interlinking modules, forming vast sequences of matter. And I tried to understand the mechanisms through which one or another structure would affect me so powerfully, for example, by formulating a plausible description of the interior of a Chinese pomegranate—the white partitions separating the seeds of the fruit, once the seeds have been dislodged, are a ductile and elastic meat with hollowed contours and sharp protuberances, separating the nests of implantation—or the walnut, with its meandering channels and inner convolutions. Interlocking spaces, chains of paired objects, the incessant combination of the concave or the convex, of geometries in which an arbitrary line drawn in pencil across a sheet of paper would turn upon itself, spontaneously merging with another line, enclosing it within its interior, then surrounded by another line reproducing, in turn, other broken lines, all in half circles, similar formations in a constantly intensifying and self-multiplying process, constituted my perpetual mania for enclosure and aperture, for diffraction and refraction of particles from what is real.

A nucleus surrounded by an immense quantity of subunits that are intercommunicated—or enclosed—by confining or liberating corridors, this was the basic structure that obsessed me and through which were directed the modulations of my sense of touch upon objects, my way of viewing paintings, and my ear for music in organizing the sounds that reached me. Fruitlessly, I tried to discern the nature of my responses to those rhythms of structure, but I remained on the surface of the phenomenon, unable to discover its mystery. The sensation produced was thus an objective state of classification within the coordinates of the human or animal species; was it perhaps symptomatic of a pathology? Maybe it was, judging by the way in which it refused to be described as a mere metaphor. Often I asked other people if they were not caused anxiety—"given to anxieties" was the term so aptly applied in Mexico to describe nervousness and uneasiness produced by certain unmanageable situations—by the ordering of honeycombs in cells, but I never found anyone who echoed my unease or who sympathized with my urgent need to understand my affliction.

I could have searched for this cellular model in various disciplines, investigated its presence in both nature and art, but nowhere would I have discovered why it overwhelmed me with such a sense of vertigo. The situation bordered on the paranoid to the extent that I found everything surrounding me to be covered by a soft film, imprisoned within an elastic, karyokinetic epithelium, and I began to realize that I, too, might become trapped within this reticular obsession.

Delicate ripples move across the electronic soundboard, slight movements produced as if someone were applying pressure to, or driving a wedge beneath, a corner of the greater mass. The cells dart from one side to the other, almost imperceptibly, and from within or beneath this sonorous element occur gentle uprisings that later explode as small volcanoes. Here and now, in this chamber, or unit, constituted by my self as well as my senses, there is no *seeing,* that is, not the common exercise of passing one's gaze over objects, but an *idea of seeing* that does not attempt to see, but, rather, it is *to hear what is seen,* to hear an interior glance or, beyond a glance, an aptitude for creating a radial board of the conscience upon which, at times, sounds light up.

Music, like an enormous respiratory pump, expels matter in radii and compresses it into knots in deliberately measured rhythms or unintentional dysrhythmia within or outside the series. Enclosed in this space, which is only real according to its allotment of virtuality, more an operative mental construct for describing the effects of music than a physical state, now *I see what I hear;* the sound waves pursue one another and, at the junctures where they meet, surround my mind or tighten over my heart, demanding my bodily accompaniment. But my body refuses to move, I am suspended inside, weightless, and yet not one appendage so much as vibrates or noticeably responds to the musical cadence. Movement, the sonorous incisions, the vibratory aftereffects abruptly dispersed at the points of intersection by the columns of sound, the fading colors, transparent and laden with values from the rising and falling scales of the composition, all of this transpires in the chamber of *seeing what I hear,* a secret factory, a compartment outside the flow of the five senses but spanning and subsuming them all through condensations as yet lacking nomenclature.

I have passed my entire life in this compartment of my persona; there, it is always night, the transition from black to gray indicates inactive moments in anticipation of the light announced through movement from side to side, from top to bottom, from east to west and north to south and, taking poetic license, through all the infinite intermediary cardinal points of my universe, sparkling white beams of light. The night is a cavity as well as my chamber where I remain with closed eyes; they both cherish and claim the same mystery; one houses or coincides with the other in a superimposition randomly designated by the cell of seeing what I hear. In the way that this alleged commando of the conscience resists revealing its true nature, I have looked for signs of the cellular effect; only there, fanned out on the perpetually nocturnal soundboard, could there ever have occurred the gentle yet biting sensation, revealing its manner of working upon my anxieties.

Left entirely to the manifestations of this body that is myself and all that pertains to me in my cellular chamber, distributed in alveolar arcs as if upon an enormous circumference subdivided by poles and diameters, thus prisoner of the geometric obsession and the endless karyokinesis that could finally pulverize reality, there, searching for an answer to the great enigma, signified taking a risk: that through perverse mediations or interstices of the unconscious, the perforated underlying surface might suddenly become persecutory and uncontrollable. Already, long ago in what must have been the fifties, through an intense night of wakefulness, I can recall that the gentle and polished sensation of thousands of tiny cavities distributed in threads within a box and destined for the implantation of something, perhaps pieces that I had never identified, cavities already emptied of those pieces, reduced my persona to a minuscule and besieged being, while the chamber expanded of its own volition as if it had assumed a threatening life of its own, independent of me and yet, paradoxically, a part of me. This compartment that included me and that was me grew beyond *our* limits, rendering me an empty shell, and all of space was filled with terror.

I could not, then, surrender myself without reservations to the unlimited manufacture of images in my hidden factory. Although those restless nights did not provide me with an explanation of the cellular effect, they constituted my principal nourishment; sporadic as they were, they limited my desire to submerge myself among them, and for long periods they remained (and remain) closed, blocking me from adventure and obliging me to control my perception. Still, despite the risk, I probed some almost forgotten scenes that could have configured the symptom; I wanted to encounter the waking dream that my good sense denied me, and the search could only take place there in the chamber with eyes closed, where my inwardly turned concentration is at a maximum and the loss of images is at a minimum.

I remembered another sensation that occurred to me during a high fever some thirty years ago: the room in which I was sleeping, superimposed as usual upon my secret fantasy chamber (or, where I see what I hear, or see what I am observing with my conscious eye, that is, the eye of my mind), the room slowly began to separate (from my secret compartment) as if some strange force were lifting it, that is, raising its armature and dividing it, rendering the walls invisible, rendering them nothing more than "wind," incorporeal, and rendering me, as a consequence, without structure, destructuring me, plainly and simply, disintegrating my self and my self/chamber.

These dangers have often frightened me in the face of my task, and I have avoided submerging myself in such shell-like situations; unable to manage them at my own discretion and pleasure, I have opted for mental health, as if that were a viable option, as if the cellular obstacle could be avoided by making a personal decision.

One day, after returning to Argentina, I decided to comb through the forbidden zones of my memory to discover, at all costs, the moment at which the surface of the cell received its sinister mark. A word occurred to me, "overcrowding," together with an effect or an action: the species is teeming, it is proliferative. And along the narrow corridor permitted me by my conscience, all alone, I encounter elaborate walls, vast and dense bas-reliefs whose soft, morbid projections and recesses seem to call out to my sense of touch. But the touch rejects what the vision increasingly defines as truth: the friezes that appear and that I recognize are the first images I ever saw and registered more than forty years ago, they are photographs of concentration camps kept by my parents. Bodies lying in mounds, all dead; bodies lying neatly aligned in open graves, appropriately called mass graves; the interior of a gas chamber, viewed in cross section (the door has been left open); the marching columns of a Nazi parade, the round helmets viewed from above, endless columns, like a rectangular box divided into squares. This order established through terror repels and at the same time devours; if it is avoided, it triumphs anyway, the cavity wins the day.

The Furtive
Species

Of a summer night in January or February of 1951, there remains but a vestige that breaks away from the story it pertains to, and, thus freed, alone and isolated, it appears like a traffic sign, fixed to other events in my life, but without any possible permanence, like an anima. The hand of a child reaches across the empty space that separates his bed from mine, boldly suspended in the darkness, cast into the void where my girlish hand is upraised and waiting; the two hands have overcome all adversity, all opposition, to simultaneously receive and transmit their mutual desire to be united. That unique, fleeting, and imperishable contact on that summer night, the chance result of the positioning of the beds and the children in those beds, in that room, at the discretion of adults, that union of hands that discovered one another, that grasped one another, producing successive interior illuminations and an ardent pain because in the intensity provoked by that union there was already the anticipation of separation, that fervent and momentary fusion established for me, irrevocably, the furtive species.

The Furtive Species

All through the day that followed, the next year, the next five years, and over the course of four more decades to come, that image gave rise to a strange brilliance that hurt, curiously, with an ever-increasing pain even as it was already being slowly extinguished, losing force, and advancing irrevocably toward extinction. The dark eyes of the boy, I remember, did not look at me when the light drew to an end that summer night; they remained hidden behind his curtainlike eyelids, and everything was preserved in the imminence of the night before. In the aftermath, all that has occurred since establishing that first bridge in the night, in the epiphany of the encounter or the sorrow of the loss, has had resonance in that figure: no matter how the image has grown in me, the other, like that child, is mute and absent when the figure itself is recreated. The species is stubbornly reproduced, especially upon my return to Argentina; it has recurred in memories and has lodged in my conscious mind like a descendant who can be neither disowned nor, for that matter, denied a name.

At times, that bridge extended into the early evening shadows is my own gaze crossing the street from behind half-drawn curtains; on the other side is a child in knickers, gray school stockings, and black ankle boots; he looks at the house, measures it with dark, penetrating, ferretlike eyes, then peers into the distance for the tram that does not come; he looks back at the house and, suddenly responding to my silent summons from the shadows, stares into the very space where I stand, he remains fixed in my pupil as a tram passes, then another, and he lingers, ensnared in the circle of my eye. His hand moves, very slightly, and he takes a step forward, as if to make a sign of having discerned my gaze that is invisible but seems to have established an

unbreakable union with his own. On another occasion, I drew
back the curtains and showed myself, and the encounter then
became evident: as he waved to me, smiling, waiting for the
tram, we were discovered by someone at another window. My
fear of censure, the bridge having been broken by the intrusion
of a third party, and my disappearance into the room obliterated
the signal, and, the emission thus curtailed, the boy in knickers
whose name was Elvio withdrew from my life, he withdrew but
he returns because without being aware of it he made contact
with the constitutive substance, the stealthy and scheming furtive species.

The furtive nature of this species has one characteristic: the
encounter, the secret nocturnal bridge, extended in the morning
or afternoon but, nonetheless, nocturnal, is an acquisition that
endures forever; it is a good that does not depreciate, but, rather,
with each renovation, its effects are reaffirmed. I have crossed
the bridge a thousand times and summoned it many more when
my life was floundering, but one night during the month of July,
in 1987, a few months after my return to Buenos Aires, it
reached out, tense, in mid-arch, suspended over an unbridgeable
void in a way that had never happened before; I and he, that necessary other, necessary so that the figure can be recreated, remained poised on the edge of the precipice, unable to cross the
intervening space, and, what is more, the awful sense of separation and loss was left hanging on my side, uncompensated.

It was then that I realized that another symptom was about to
appear, the same as in other moments of my life when earth and
sky would draw apart, leaving me unprotected, another symptom of the divided self. I did not have to go back very far in time
in order to recapture it: only a few years before, that door to

vulnerability had been left open and I had inadvertently passed through it. I hesitate to recount it, but the image obstinately imposes itself as if, for some reason, the episode had to take precedence in this text over the sense of alienation associated with the furtive species. It was in a hotel, the night of my arrival in London, two days before conducting some interviews that I and a North American photographer had been sent to do for a Mexican magazine. She was dressed like a Vietnam veteran, in olive-green jacket, pants, and army boots; I wore cotton clothing on a day in April that, in fact, was colder than the worst August I had ever known during my life in the Southern Hemisphere. Walking through Hyde Park, I took short steps like those of a lapwing, while my companion stomped along with the elastic strides of a goose. As we passed the different groups scattered about the park—Islamics, fundamentalists, Indians, or Pakistanis—I experienced the mounting sensation of physical shrinkage, almost a negation of my person, as I made an effort to keep up with my colleague, who had the enormous advantage of knowing the language, although, being a North American in England, it became increasingly evident that people did not understand her; it was as if her inadequacy somehow compensated for my sense of inferiority, as we walked along the paths of Hyde Park.

On one of the sidewalks outside the park, a number of people were avidly following the movements of the police, who had surrounded the Iranian embassy, occupied by hostage-holding terrorists. Once inside the park, but still at a distance, I saw a gathering of people around an enormous Mexican flag; the green, red, and white fabric fluttered in the air, and that gentle patriotic motion was like a mating call beckoning to me, fugitive and immoderate Argentine, forever possessed by the covetous and impossible desire to be Mexican. That fluttering flag in the distance was my shroud of tears on that frozen afternoon in Hyde Park. I even felt that I was gaining a slight advantage over my photographer companion, who in Mexico was just as much a foreigner as I, but I reminded myself that it is one thing to be a South American in Mexico and quite another to be from the United States, and I hurried ahead, self-assured, toward the waving flag. What unspeakable horror it was for me when I discovered that in place of the eagle posed upon the nopal cactus, the flag had at its center an imperial lion, terrible and majestic, and, what is more, surrounding the national symbol were people who spoke a language that was quite unknown to me.

This revelation, my futile headlong rush, and my inappropriate cotton clothing in the freezing spring had all been brewing in advance during my overseas journey: terror and vulnerability were seeds planted by an episode that occurred in the rear seat of the airplane just a few minutes before our stopover in Bermuda. We had seen a stewardess hurrying down the aisle, responding to a call. Without making a fuss, in a mute scene, she leaned over a traveler seated by the window and confirmed that he was dead; the traveler's wife had not said a word, not even a whimper or a sob issued from her lips; she and the stewardess, it might be imagined, had sealed a discretionary pact to politely abandon the man to his fate. When we landed, there was already an ambulance waiting on the runway: the lost island was receiving a dead foreigner.

Upon our arrival at the hotel where reservations had been made for us, passing through the door to my room, I found an immense platter heaped with fruit on a low table surrounded by armchairs: fresh bunches of grapes, apples, pears, plums, and oranges; this enumeration, mind you, does not necessarily obey strict descriptive rules; in that moment, I do not think I would have paid much attention to the species of fruit in the dish. I do know that I did not dare eat so much as a single grape and that, along with that act of self-denial, I began to think and even to say aloud a sentence that at first was merely tentative: "someone has committed suicide in a London hotel . . . who committed suicide in a London hotel?" as if expecting an answer from someone present in the room, in one of those dialogues that take place in the absence of communication. "Someone committed suicide in a London hotel," I repeated, "someone committed suicide in a London hotel," and in order to escape from that sentence whose intensity was becoming intolerable, I turned on the television, and there on the screen appeared a scene right out of a story, perhaps *La Cenerentola,* and the peachy color of the images, on top of the voice that went on repeating that someone had committed suicide in a London hotel, filled me with terror, so I changed the channel and found that just at that moment elite troops were retaking the embassy from the hostage-holding Iranians, and I watched a commando leap from a cornice to a window, and there were clouds of smoke from the grenades that lingered in the air for a few minutes before dissipating, like flowers of death, and I rid myself of that image, trying to recompose my lucidity, but the phrase came back, demanding an answer. I telephoned the photographer in her room, but she was unable to respond to my need: not only did I plead for help, but I also asked her who had committed suicide in a London hotel. Unfortunately, she was just at that moment taking enormous strides into the realm of dreams, so I did not succeed in keeping her awake, and she said, almost in a whisper: "I can't . . . I can't take anymore, I can't do anything for you, I'm falling asleep, I took my pills and they're taking effect, I have to go, I have to go . . . ," and her voice faded off and disappeared. Defeated, I too lay down on my bed, and finally the answers began to come to me in tandem: I had committed suicide in a London hotel, I have committed suicide in a London hotel, she commits suicide in a London hotel, and I said these words over and over until I saw that woman, until I saw myself, wrapped in a bathrobe, together with a platter of fruit glowing in the darkness and a television screen with luminous reflections like grenade explosions and distant blasts of machine-gun fire in the vicinity of Hyde Park and a flag with an imperial lion emblazoned upon its center waving in defiance of all historic or geographic previsions. I do not know which remnants of myself survived that long prayer, murmured perhaps in the same tone as the words whispered by the stewardess into the ears of the dead man and the words of the man's wife in the last row of the airplane.

The furtive species, along with the divided self, has a discernible construction: an interior voice, slightly separated from my own and forming a kind of aura of sound around itself, says to me, in unexpected circumstances, a truth. Sometimes this truth is expressed in the form of a doubt, as in the case of the frantic need for information about the person who committed suicide in a London hotel. On other occasions, the truth is expressed sharply and directly, interrupting a period of luxurious tranquility, saying, *don't think that this is going to last forever, you know perfectly well that there is always death.* The phrase closes gently on the final word, *death,* as a matter of conscience, of moral resistance, becoming blurred in its effort to be reasonable but emerging with a systematically and increasingly clear and perfect deline-

ation: *don't think that this is going to last forever*, in the first half of
the sentence like a simple conditioner relativizing a state that
could be considered perpetual, a sort of wise taking of distance,
but that deals a harsh blow in the second half, a *death* blow, allowing no time for sidestepping but striking hard and laying me
low. And later, little by little, the sentence travels to a third person, a *she* who should know that not everything is going to be as
it has been up until then but, rather, that there is always death,
she defending herself through different pronominal usages, as if,
without noticing, she had been robbed of her identity, ricochet-
ing from *you* to *I* and from there back to *she,* in a dangerous
game of seductions, each oblivious of the others, each absorbed
in its own strategy for emerging with the maximum whispered
truth at hand.

In July of 1987, the voice was transformed into an image: a
man, perhaps an artist, and the more the image emerged as a
person, the more it resembled a musician, someone I had lost
but whose face I was not permitted to see. In my conscious
mind, or, to put it another way, in that twilight zone where these
types of revelations take place and where exploration is not permitted for normal everyday kinds of reasoning, he apparently
had "created me out of a puff of air"—that was the idea—and I
had allowed myself to be rolled along, so to speak, by that puff
of air and had been transformed by a whim of that pneuma. The
man playing the double bass watched me from a stage to the
right of the orchestra, the deep notes rebounding in all directions; its succinct phrase told me that I had lost him, and this
produced a disastrous effect on me. I wanted to rationalize, to
take inventory of the musicians; I searched for whoever was
playing the bassoon, the trumpet, the drums, but no, the bass

insidiously played on, imposing itself like an absent presence, crumbling all notions of reality because he was saying, in his subworld phrases, that he had abandoned me.

Once I had accepted the pain of having lost him, this other person's existence became even more real to me, almost converted into flesh and blood, although I never had any actual relations with him, not even in my remotest fantasies. The weaving of this story had been something independent of me and my circumstance and in a devious way had invaded my interior, my mind, my soul and, suddenly, without any warning, had caused me great suffering and a sense of loss. It was as if I had been in a house one night, in a meandering conversation almost without objectives and without any consciousness of mental, spiritual, libidinal, or amorous substance, and my interlocutor, without making a sound or movement, had inoculated me and invaded my space. It was months or years later when I realized with dismay that I had lost him without ever having treasured him and that it was useless to try to get him back as a person of flesh and blood, much less to summon his actual presence: he could only be present in the way that he had branded me: furtively and surreptitiously.

The Guided
Visit

Pedro, a Spanish refugee of rather diffused nationality, somewhere between French and central European, "stuck" to the Argentines, so to speak, though it could just as well have been to the Uruguayans or the Chileans, and made himself one of the group. We had the impression that in this way he was carrying out a kind of emotional exercise, putting to the test the old traumas that marked his existence; he was reviving a system of reflexes of solidarity and fusion with outcasts, a system he had grown up with.

He would not tell the story of what had turned him into such a susceptible and obsessive being, but it was known that when he was seven years old, with the world at war, his parents had been forced to leave Paris hurriedly during the occupation because their work of helping refugees had attracted the attention of the Germans. One early morning, the mother and child left the city, setting off in one direction, while the father set off in another. The first two rode a bus toward the south along routes infested with checkpoints. At one of these stops, near some woods, the mother and some other volunteers offered to go down to the river for water. The child, watching his mother walk away along a path, must have seen how the sunlight lit on her back as she disappeared from his sight. A few minutes later, even before those left waiting in the bus could grow impatient from the delay, a German plane came along, strafing the roadway; it was not a devastating attack, but the driver panicked and drove off toward the south with the remaining passengers on board, abandoning those who had gone in search of water.

The child arrived in the south and was interned in a refugee camp for orphans, although he had not been orphaned; incorporated into the long columns of internees (the typical concentration camp situation), he was submitted to the dictates of his German tutors: he stood in line to receive his bowl of food, to use the toilet, to go to the playground, to cross the village in order to use the public baths. On one of those occasions, when they had scarcely begun the march through the streets, he slipped out of line and sneaked into a house; the column moved on down the street, and no one noticed his absence. Taken in by the household, his name was incorporated into the lists of names of those who were lost and those who had been found, and, several months later, when the consequences of the disappearances were already irreparable, the mother found her son, mute, pale, trembling, and frightened, never having come to accept any of the assurances and explanations that his protectors had used in order to allay his fears. Sometime later, not just two or three days, or even weeks, but several months afterward, mother and child took a train in order to somehow reach a ship that was leaving for Mexico, without ever having heard from or about the missing father; in the middle of the night, the convoy made a rest stop in the countryside, and this time Pedro got off the train with his mother in order to find some water. They stood in a line and, to their surprise, and indeed it was extraordinary, among those serving the water stood the father. Such meetings are almost never so perfect, nor is the line of trajectory so perfect: the layout of the roads, the search for water in the woods, the formations of German planes, the strafing of the roads, the mother separated from the vehicle, the route traveled toward the south, the column marching through the streets of the village toward the public baths, the child who escapes, the reunion of mother and child, the voyage resumed by train, the line for receiving water, the reappearance of the father, the end of the cycle. However, the apparent happy ending with the family reunited was not such a complete and unconditional success in mitigating the damage to the child, or to the father, or, moreover, to the mother. Pedro spent the rest of his life waiting for his mother, who had left him to go in search of water, and she continued to search for her son, who had gone on without her toward the south.

Pedro met with the Argentines regularly and systematically; he lived as all pariahs do, stabilized in his own personal void, inclined to regenerate the void whenever possible by filling it with some kind of expectation; he always found new opportunities for reaffirming it because he never stopped correcting and rectifying. Nothing was ever complete for him, nothing was perfect or fair, and thus he went through life saying *no* to whoever affirmed, saying *yes* to whoever negated, centering whatever moved to the right or to the left, looking for error or discrepancy in whatever passed before his eyes or fell into his hands, and altogether converting these characteristics into elements that opposed his own smooth insertion into the world. To step out of line, to transgress the limits, to lose sight of reality and go beyond the point of no return can lead one to obsession, insanity, or artistry, or all three things at once. Pedro's fate was to be an artist.

Perhaps he joined us because re-creation of the void was the characteristic condition of living in exile: deficiency, compensation for deficiency; nakedness and clothing, mutilation and prosthesis, and our exile was, so to speak, fresh, recently premiered, receptive and, therefore, for the veteran Spanish experience and, at the same time, for our Spanish friend, a fertile ground for the exercise of lack. For the same reasons that he was drawn to us, we were drawn to other exiles like ourselves, and, beginning with those most distant from us in the chronology of exile, we banded together with the Guatemalans, and from there on down the line until we reached the Chileans and Uruguayans. In our particular case, mine and those dearest to me, the ultimate model of tragedy and dramatically interrupted exile was Leon Trotsky, and it was to him that we were drawn, almost without being aware of it, although we sensed that it was only through such extreme cases that some meaning could be grasped, the key to understanding this condition in which we found ourselves included.

It is a fact that every Argentine whose politics are on the left, and perhaps it could be said of all people who define themselves in terms that include some degree of socialism, never fail to visit Leon Trotsky's house on Vienna Street, in Coyoacán, and they will not feel at ease until they have been there, passing through the rooms haunted by a certain asceticism, revolution, or death, in which one breathes the air of one of the most melancholy atmospheres on earth. To visit Leon Trotsky's house is a kind of initiation rite, and one has the impression that only there does personal experience reach historic and collective dimensions.

Having recently arrived in Mexico, we went to Leon Trotsky's house in November of 1974; we returned in January of 1975, and again in March of that same year, and then once every two or three months for almost the next five years, carrying out various rituals each time: the first time we, my loved ones and I, put our signatures in a guest book that would subsequently be nourished by dozens of inscriptions and slogans left by other Argentines upon their arrival in Mexico who unknowingly signed a pact, as we had, with the greatest of all exiles and with his vulnerability.

We would go on Saturdays or Sundays, pull the cord of an invisible bell, and there would appear one or another militant in the doorway—for a time, it was an Argentine—who lived there and was in charge of caring for the house-museum. We would sit by the tombs of Leon Davidovich and his wife, Natalia Sedova, covered with flowering violets or luxuriant clover, according to the season. We would take our dog with us; one of us would stay outside with him while the others entered the house; first we would browse through the newspapers in all different languages announcing, in bold headlines, the assassination; we would read and reread those pages that, the first time we went, were laid out in the open but, later, were put under transparent plastic for protection, and every time we looked through them the tragedy was repeated; we would read them as if reading Shakespeare, knowing the outcome in advance, but nonetheless feeling an intense anguish, as if just learning the news for the first time. From this room we would pass to the next, where there was a table and some wicker chairs and the remains—or, perhaps, that was all there was at the time, taking into account the austerity of the Trotskys—of some furniture typical of an eat-in kitchen, including various Mexican plates and utensils. Re-creating the atmosphere toward the end of the 1930s, we could imagine a group of people gathered around the table, between five and six o'clock in the afternoon on just about any day, with tea being served and announced to the houseguests by Natalia Sedova.

The next room, adjoining the dining room through a doorway, was Trotsky's study, the desk covered every time we visited by transparent plastic through which were visible his glasses, his papers, an old cylindrical recorder, and a telephone, that desk at which he was attacked and upon which he fell, in that crime that has been reconstructed innumerable times and without exaggeration in police blotters and in human memory. We then passed to the bedroom, with the beds exactly as they were at the time, bookshelves filled with books in Russian and other languages; the walls scarred by the spray of machine-gun bullets fired by Siqueiros and his band that, it might be imagined, forced the Trotskys to throw themselves to the floor, beside the beds. Finally, we passed through the last of the interconnecting doorways, as if, one by one, we were joining the seasons of a temporal cycle, and we would pause to contemplate the magnitude of the assault, for it was a heavily armored door; it led to the bedroom of Leon Trotsky's grandson, and its opening was smaller than that of the other doors; to the right, in the bathroom, in a kind of dressing room, we could always see and touch some articles of clothing belonging to the Trotskys, abandoned in that closet without doors, left behind, no less, in their natural tomb. As we passed from room to room we would reconfirm that every detail was still in place, that the last apparent traces of

The Guided Visit

Trotsky remained the same beneath our gaze and touch; yet, if we were to repeat the tour that same day or on a subsequent visit, some new detail would always appear. In that house, most impressive for what was lacking, for its dispossession and desiccation, for its absolute and militant rigor, things grew and multiplied, the senses proliferated and adhered to an angle of a room, a piece of paper, the spine of a book, the decadent life and exalted death of the atmosphere in that space.

The visits to the house of L. T. were quite long. We would suddenly realize that more than thirty or forty minutes had passed while we were inside, not counting the time we spent in the garden with the dog and the children near the old rabbit cages or by the tombs over which the red flag emblazoned with the hammer and sickle waved, and when we turned homeward it would be rather late: those were the final hours of peaceful Sundays, with a perspective of grayish time and hours that crushed one's heart, for the impregnation produced by that story created in us, without surfacing to our consciousness, a dense fusion of various nostalgias.

Much time has transpired since those visits, and reviewing them now allows me to see more clearly just how much the figure of L. T. was tutelary, with just how much force its very meaning sealed the fissures through which meaning itself could have escaped. This "communing" with him was not a matter of assimilation of a representative character: it was not a specialization, nor an immersion in partisan terminology, processes that would have culminated, logically, in a succinct adhesion to the cause of the Fourth International; nor was there worship, or revision, or rectification of anything historical in these acts. L. T. was simply converted into one of my own, a loved one who had won over our consciences, our working days and holidays, our Wednesdays, Fridays, Saturdays, and Sundays during that period of exile.

One night, in the late hours, my daughter, who was eight or nine at the time, awoke several times suffering and complaining of the same recurring nightmare, and each time we went to her bedside to soothe her she said the same thing: *I dreamed that we couldn't get out of Trotsky's house.* The dream and the phrase were repeated on numerous nights during the course of numerous months. *I dreamed that we were all in Trotsky's house, with the dog, and we couldn't get out* was the leitmotif, and we thought at the time, as the vertigo of the thought swallowed us up, that the phrase condensed the entire history and destiny of the Left over the last forty years, our history and our destiny.

Our attraction to the house of L. T. and its consequences were not original: C. A., another exile, had lived almost fifteen years in Mexico, and every day, also moved by a similar fixation, he would go to the house and remain there for long hours; he knew all of the press clippings by heart and had even tried to become the house-museum's caretaker and guardian. In the afternoons he would climb the lookout tower above the "bunker," a strong word he used in reference to the house in which he would have liked to live, a word that seemed to have a dry, lethal resonance, and he would stare at the horizon between the buildings and the trees of Coyoacán, imbued with the early evening sadness of any sentinel in his watchtower. This rapport between the man and his environment, proverbial for all revolutionaries of the species, impregnated the will and intellect of C. A. and led him through a series of explorations and crises during his years of militancy in the ranks of Trotskyism and, over time, into exile.

The Guided Visit

The visits to Vienna Street became increasingly spaced apart; the children and the dog no longer accompanied us. It was necessary to strip those visits of their cemetery-like character and to avoid, likewise, a second stage that usually completed the ritual. The circuit had an annex to it, a sort of second movement, almost compensatory, which involved going to the house of Frida Kahlo, where she and Diego Rivera had lived for a period, although we did not know at first that the Trotskys had lived there too, since there are no indications or references to the fact, and that the Dewey hearings had also been held there. That house-museum, also suspended in time, with the objects and anima of the people still present, with furniture and articles still charged and vibrating with their energy, had something sinister about it. I do not know why I repeated that "circuit" through the garden and the bedrooms so often, ending up in Frida's studio and in the presence of that horrible portrait of Stalin that remains on the easel, were it not to find traces of my own formation: war in Spain, world war, Nazism, concentration camps, Stalinism, secret police, abject confessions, defeats and hopes, and that halo of those decades in which I was born and grew up. Every time I entered those houses, the first on Vienna Street, the second on Allende Street, both in Coyoacán, I felt that I was entering a very distant and imaginary "paternal" house that, leaping the decades, had transmigrated to offer me shelter.

Houses

We could not escape from the house of Leon Trotsky, and, at the same time, just as I had been unable to wear a legitimate piece of my own clothing due to some strange sort of ablation, I seemed to lack the drive necessary for adapting to a new home or, more accurately, for accepting the house I was living in as my home. For as long as I can remember and for reasons I could not understand, this obliterated desire rendered the sensation of being alive totally provisional, without roots, without fixation to objects, dispossessed of the logic of appropriation that is common to human beings. As much as I tried to stay put in the places where I was compelled to live, I was forever on the move; there was an internal time limit that left me no margin for settling myself into any one place; this time limit was always being deferred, given that I remained in many places for long periods of time, but this did not imply inaction: I would arrive, I would orient myself with ease; within hours of my arrival I would already be arranging the tables, the chairs, putting things on the walls, in the drawers, on the shelves, but despite this instantaneous settling in, something mysterious still prevented my feeling that *I was there,* that the ordered space was really my home.

For a time I was assaulted, both night and day, by a certain anxiety that I came to associate—as is almost always the case—with a particular phrase. On that occasion the phrase was *Nothing around me belongs to me.* And, in truth, as I looked at the objects around me, the furniture, the beds, the books, I understood, clearly and irrefutably, that nothing of what was in that house was really mine. I could not rid myself of that anxiety, and as much as I touched those objects, telling myself in a loud voice, *this is mine,* and mustering up a sense of possession, nothing came of it. Not even my loved ones seemed to really belong to me, and, what is more, I felt they were even less mine as they tried to convince me that everything around us was, in fact, mine and theirs, it was all ours and had been acquired through the force and very existence of us all, and yet they could not rescue me from my sense of estrangement. No matter that I would organize, plant, furnish, arrange things, fill all the empty spaces with my being, my objects; I always had this feeling that nothing belonged to me and that everything was provisional.

There were dozens of anecdotes referring to the same precarious and rootless state, and when I told them to an analyst, as usual outside of treatment, she gave me no solutions. Rather, as if referring to a phase in my evolution, she told me that at this time in my life it could be stated, without margin for error, that this precarious and provisory life was perhaps *what corresponded to the form of my desire,* a phrase that I have nurtured ever since and that has enabled me to live my life according to the form of my desire, taking full advantage of the fatalistic notion of destiny that the phrase implies. From that moment on, the provisional

Houses

house in which I have been living—whatever its geographic location might be—the house that has contained me and contained my being, my existence, my essence, that has *planted itself* in this world and spread its base far and wide, that house has been a kind of launch pad for me.

The houses dreamed of in nightmares, however, would not go away in response to that quaint palliative phrase. The house of my childhood in Córdoba, for instance, would appear in my dreams, perforated by doorless closets where I stood, trapped amid the quivering silks, cottons, and woolens. From my crib, in one of the remotest rooms, I watched the play of light and shadow during my nap and was filled with terror; in another, not so distant in time, I saw a mirror from my bed in which a pair of eyes were reflected, as if someone were sitting behind me, watching over me like a guardian angel, yet frightening me so that my prayers for soothing company, said before going to sleep, were self-defeating. I dreamed that in the kitchen of that house there was a great cage filled with fluttering birds hanging from the ceiling; the cage had no bottom; nonetheless the birds crashed against the bars, unable to escape, condemned to remain in their prison.

The house reduplicated its spaces, the walls loomed upward, and the ceiling hollowed and tapered like an inverted funnel through which my best energies escaped. Imprisoned in that house, my dreams transported me back and forth, tearing me away in successive relocations, and I, like my daughter in her nightmare, could not escape: it was a vast sphere in whose interior I was condemned to drift for all eternity; it was a coffin, a ship, an aerial paradise.

Houses

Later, we turned our thoughts toward the house of our return, the house we would occupy once back in Argentina. It became evident that, after thirteen years, our Buenos Aires house of 1974 was lost to us and that the memory of that house could evoke the memory of all the previous houses we had abandoned. It was then that the transhumance and dispossession struck us in all its magnitude, like statistics of a reality that had previously been ignored. All our furniture was gone; at a distance we had been unable to locate a single blanket, sheet, mirror, rug, or knife, and we had only a dozen trunks containing our books and papers.

In my new nightmares the future house was erected: it was always unfinished, the rooms always had doors that opened to other unexplored rooms, yet to be incorporated, and that potential house continued to grow beyond its real walls, inviting me to wander down dark hallways, to ascend stairways that would suddenly end, like the galleries of existence itself, and the rooms were then left in a state of isolation, out of order and out of series, but they were attractive because I imagined that they contained all of our lost objects and furniture.

The house we were to buy was located on a large site in the vacant lots of my unconscious; it promised wings facing east and west, temporarily folded up and awaiting extension. In the dream, every corner had a vast beyond, and the promise of that vastness was as distressing as it was delightful. The first of these dreamed-up residences was set in a shady but not somber bend of a dead-end street among old buildings; it was a two-story dwelling of pink quarry stone. The second was in the heart of a city block, and its closed spaces, once opened, led to the void.

But the moment arrived when the house forged in my fantasy

Houses

gave way to reality. The house was there waiting for us, an apartment this time, already acquired for our occupancy upon our arrival in Argentina, and thus it departed from my dreams and projections. Even so, I still dreamed of the house, and a recurring
force shaped the reiterated modular structure in my nightmare:
the unexplored rooms only contained terror, and this terror in-
creased as the moment of our moving into them drew near. Even
now, after years of living in the apartment, I still discover upon
waking that I have been aware of the vague muffled noises of a
secret life behind closed doors or that I have perceived a summons from within the spaces between the walls and the alcove,
an intermediate space giving notice of another reality.

Embassy

G eneral Menéndez walks the streets of Córdoba; this phrase, as part of the account reported to me by someone who had just returned from Argentina, upset me terribly and left me in shock: for the first time in all my years of exile, for the first time since I had left Córdoba in the decade of the sixties, I felt that I was trapped, from afar, in a global and synthetic category that included, in blacks, whites, and grays, my entire past. The narrator added: *And without guaruras,* which is the term used in Mexico for bodyguards. *General Menéndez walks the streets of Córdoba, and without bodyguards,* that said it all. How could General Menéndez walk the streets of Córdoba when the vote had *already* been taken and the military leaders had been publicly condemned everywhere in the country?

General Menéndez walked through my city, and as he advanced along the streets, he displaced, cast aside, not to say eliminated, my father's footsteps. There was not enough room for the two of them. My father moved through the streets like a ship, serene, without trepidation, advancing quickly, not out of haste, but as a simple matter of habit. That ominous image of

Embassy

the general, with or without retinue, strutting along 9 de Julio
Street as far as Olmos and then turning into Colón, entering the
building of the Jockey Club in the face of the whole world's pas-
sivity, which came to supplant the image of my father in such a
grotesque and intimidating way, was a synthesis of Argentina,
and not only of the Argentina of terror that we all thought had
come to an end, but the current and enduring Argentina. The
contrasting image that the phrase stirred up began to hound me:
my father in the streets of Córdoba, pausing on various occasions along his way to greet and be greeted by various people
while we, his children, followed some feet behind in the wake of
his brisk footsteps. And there was that second, ferocious scene
of the general that caused the adrenaline to roil within me and
the emotional gastric pain I suffered precisely as a result of my
father's death in Córdoba two years before, during my absence,
because I was living ten thousand kilometers to the north.

We resorted to various ways of venting our hatred and dissatis-
faction when assailed by such images as those described above.
One way was to go to the Argentine embassy in Mexico, then
located on the Paseo de la Reforma, the section crossing
through Lomas, to wave our banners inscribed with antimilitary
slogans and, from there, standing in the middle of the boule-
vard, or up on the traffic island, to shout insults or make hostile
gestures. The building was always closed, but that people were
inside was evident from the trembling of the curtains or traces
of sound emanating from the building's interior; our clamor intensified whenever such signs were perceived, for we supposed
that we were being carefully and rigorously photographed.

Embassy

Few in number and varied in composition, entire families sat with their children on the edge of the traffic island. The group was viewed curiously by Mexicans driving by, people of comfortable means who had the habit of observing popular demonstrations but not quite understanding the clamor of these people who were very much like themselves, mostly white and blond-haired, launching threats and predicting the downfall of the military regime. Among this crowd there was always Clara Gertel—and her image must have figured among the photographs taken by those career-oriented, or temporary, diplomats of the dictatorship—who stood in the front line, among the children, and extracted from her purse the only two photos she had left of her two disappeared children; they were very small pictures, identification-card size, which she could scarcely hold between her index finger and thumb, but she brandished them without hesitation, always in the same spot, always in silence, held up to the hidden faces crouching behind embassy windows.

Another mother, Laura Bonaparte, carried placards, one for each of her disappeared sons, sons-in-law, daughters, daughters-in-law, and her husband, who had been tortured to death; they were so many, her dead, that she had to hold them up in turns, or distribute the portraits among six different people, until she finally opted to make and hold up one large placard inscribed with just the last name of her exterminated family. She must have been another strange sight for the people who went along Lomas in their automobiles, and the disturbance that our rally caused in the traffic must have been diminished somewhat by the sheer magnitude of the horror that she represented: a tall woman, beautiful, impassive, surrounded by others, at the center of a tragedy, defying the photographers who snapped our pictures from inside the embassy. That mother, Laura Bonaparte, performed one of the more significant political acts of the final years of the military regime: in an act of extreme political protest, she chained herself to one of the pillars of the Argentine consulate building on election day when we were all required to go there and have our passports stamped in a kind of abrupt and ridiculous legal formality.

Those years of depredation, which passed in a whirl of confusion, weakened or hardened the hearts and wills of many, being both one and the same thing; this weakening and hardening were both signs of the vulnerability of our emotions. The rallies outside the embassy were obviously cathartic, but, in the long run, they proved to be pathetic recourses; from year to year, or every six months, this discharge and the illusion that we were fighting the dictatorship were a political ritual that compensated for the lack, through sheer dearth, of an effective political practice. Nonetheless, the gregarious impulse to protest did not cease, and this was one of the reflexes that would remain vital in many Argentines who later returned to the country. As if they were fulfilling a sacred vow, out of a need for approbatory sanction, on their first, second, and definitive returns, they all converged on the Plaza de Mayo to march with the *Madres,* the mothers, and it was on this site, the quintessential site of the polis, as well as the tragedy of the polis, where many who had set off on different routes of exile were reunited and thus could be seen embracing one another, people who had returned from Brazil, Spain, Sweden, or Venezuela. This was the beginning— when two or three turns around the plaza could not provide a sense of closure—of the long retelling of what had happened during those intervening years, and the recognition of the other,

Embassy

the peer who had fled into exile, now a kind of mutant among compatriots who had remained in the country.

Later on, I must say, when the long hoped for integration had taken place, that satisfying *being back* that the country offered with all its cottony imperfections, the site of the polis began to fade as the object of our desires. The stinger we had brandished upon our return, with which we wished to exact vengeance upon our enemy, slowly lost its sting, and continues to lose its sting, and there remains no other intention than that of occupying the reconquered space.

culture shock

Container

———❧———

Through some unsuspected crack, in a bottomless dump, seeps the substance that defined the exiled person as an Argentine. When one imagines the return of the exiles and the reception they were given by that motherland that had cruelly sent them into exile, one generally has an erroneous idea of the nature of that reception: there was no prescribed norm for the welcome, and if it was expressed as goodwill toward the returnee, as such, it was nothing more than a formality. The exile knew beforehand that it would be difficult to "adapt," which is the all-purpose term already used from long before, when they first arrived in the country of their exile, the term that was present in all the conversations, out of anguish or eagerness to simplify, in trying to define the new situation. To ask someone if they have adapted is a cliché used by an entire social class seeking to ease its conscience. It always bothered me when I was asked that question, and it bothered me even more when I was asked: "And the children, have they adapted?" because the question presupposes that a person is like malleable putty that yields to circumstances merely by softening up. The question is ano-

the going home culture shock.

dyne, but one rarely has the urge to meet it with a sharp remark or a refusal to answer, and all exiles upon arriving in their adopted country, and then, back again in their own country, have had to begin by saying: "Well, at first my family and I, et cetera, et cetera . . . ," dividing into temporal segments a process that, by virtue of its drama, does not permit scaling down. And each person will spin their own tale: there was a before, of insufficient assimilation, and then a subsequent improvement. And within this scheme, the curious listener will have understood only what was necessary to understand, and nothing more, and the conversation can go on or end without having left any lasting impression.

The returning exile is obliged to divide the experience into periods and intensities: "at first it was hard . . . but then we got used to it," and when they finish this phrase, or this construction that refers to an advance or regression, a positive or negative state of being, they know that they have let themselves be trapped into insignificance, that they have adapted to a requirement, that they have adapted to an environment, and being a strange element in this environment, they have hidden their strangeness by employing a strategy of division into stages; there will be a future time of adaptation in which everything will be ordered in a satisfactory way.

For those who fled, the country could not reabsorb them as if they were prodigal sons and daughters; there is no precept in this sense: no person, organism, or institution has ever taken into account people who have been absent, estranged, or fugitive from reality, and much less could anyone begin to understand the psychological condition of the exile; they will always be maladjusted, asocial individuals whose emotional lives, like

Container

those of prisoners, the ill, or the alienated, will preserve their damaged circuitry, and their wounds will not be stanched upon their simple return. For those who return, the country is not an open container, and it is futile for them to try to lose themselves within the existing structures; there are no cubby holes to slip into, no houses in which to hide.

The sense of foreignness hurls itself at the returning exile; it is as if the entire person, their body and psyche, were swaddled in a membrane separating them from the world. This membrane has a buffering effect: things no longer have their former, normal weight and density, and they keep their distance from the subject in question, the mutant element in the structure. The alteration is manifest in their spatial notions, their mental ordering of the rhythms of the city, their perception of people's attitudes in the street, and in the responses they must make to neither obstruct nor collide. The idea they once had of the air, the wind, the rain, and the singing of birds has suffered a transformation during the years of absence, and everything now appears, in the best of all cases, surrounded by an aura of the unknown and the inaugural, but it may also deteriorate and become, in addition to distant, quite alien.

Returning involves a long period, that of evocation, marked by signs that appear at every turn, as if a mass of meanings were just waiting for someone to stumble into them and to set off an irrepressible, explosive, chain reaction. One steps into the street in a state of memory, either having blocked memory out or having left it at liberty to grasp the substance of reality. It is very difficult to protect that substance from the generalities of the law and to singularize it: there are exiles who return to their neighborhoods and sigh, there are those who delightedly recognize the places where their lives once took place and want to speak, at all costs, of their sensations, there are those who remain paralyzed by an odor or a taste and are enchanted by the literary image that has successfully captured those exceptional moments for all eternity, and there are those who foist their cumbersome memories onto those around them but immediately become impatient when others, like themselves, wish to carry out their own exercise of recovery.

They speak of the container that is soon to arrive, the container that was stored away, with their sights set on its reinstallation and adaptation, but also of trunks that withstood numerous attacks: pillaged by the repressors and the lucre charged by those who so kindly guarded those possessions. The conversations are plagued by trunks that have been opened and by sudden discoveries that are always significant, for anything less would be impossible, their lives having been put on hold, the revelatory potential of life intensified.

For us also, my loved ones and me, there were trunk-coffins, or Pandora's boxes. First, a trunk was sent to Mexico with some very personal effects, the family photos (so often missing, I have been told, from the trunks other people sent abroad and that were then the cause of countless psychological imbalances). The trunks that were not sent out of the country were transported from one storage location to another, creating inconveniences for the well-meaning people who concerned themselves with their protection: one day the army marched in and ransacked them, convinced that they contained arms; they only contained uncensored papers, and, despite the explanations provided, our friends were subjected to interrogations and pressures that

Container

obliged them to leave the country for a period. But the trunks remained in storage, waiting.

I opened them upon my return to Argentina. Many weeks later I began to feel the effects of that act: nightmares, emptiness, vertigo; the messages I received after opening them began, little by little, to secrete doses of anguish. I say it was the trunks because my unconscious mind worked without respite and took on the form, if I may venture the comparison, of a kind of human cavern, with back walls and false walls that stole from, and played mortal tricks upon, my conscious mind; prey to the most primary sentiments, which are of terror in the face of the unexpected and also of terror in the face of what one has already lived through, I resisted, unsuccessfully, the image that predominated: an open box allowing a glimpse into, or the escape of, the teeming reality contained within.

One of the most emotionally charged episodes of my first exploratory return to Argentina began with an irrepressible impulse: to visit my old elementary school in Córdoba. Just at the hour of my visit, the children of the afternoon shift were being let out, and, in a kind of sick out-of-body experience—in any case, quite pathetic—I believed myself to be one of the children and fell in line behind them, and in that brief, strange interval, which must have lasted only a few seconds, time shifted back to 1947. Reality has a tendency to accompany these hallucinations, giving them a false verisimilitude. When the boys and girls had all gone, spilling across the plaza Colón and along the sidewalks in the direction of Alberdi and downtown, I experienced a sudden rush of panic. Scarcely had I recovered my identity, which had practically evaporated in this flash of memory, when I saw

descending the school's sweeping staircase, with its pretensions
to stateliness, a gray-haired woman who came toward me calling my name; I responded, likewise, pronouncing her name. She
was señorita Olga Díaz, my fourth grade teacher. Neither she
nor I spoke of temporal questions; evidently she was not surprised by this meeting of two generations, nor was she perturbed by the absolute present in which she believed herself to
be speaking to me. Very confused, I let her walk away, then I
went up to the first floor; in the first bend to the right of the
corridor, I leaned out of a window. In the courtyard I saw the
same tree, a *palo borracho,* that I had seen so many times before
without admiring it as it deserved; I sensed that something very
powerful was pulling me from behind, a pressure upon the nape
of my neck that forced me to turn my head: from the classroom
for first-year high school students, just at that moment, at that
solitary hour of the day when only a school can seem so desolate
due to the absence of students, one of my former classmates,
now one of the teachers, was leaving. She asked me what I was
doing there, as if she had discovered me engaged in some kind of
profane ritual. In the time it took for me to realize that she had
not come from some other world and that I, for my part, was
still in this world, there passed a horrific, deathly moment.

   That incursion back into the fifties opened doors for my understanding of certain scenes whose basic nature could have
been useful for my utopian psychological treatment. In that
stroll through the corridors of the school with the deserted
classrooms, the same desks with their porcelain inkwells fitted
into the upper-right-hand corners and the cubbyholes beneath,
harboring the secret life of my childhood, the same geography
room with the tattered maps and gleaming, well-worn globe of

the earth, the multiresources room, the music room, and the in-
firmary, I was permitted to reclaim a scene that had been
blurred by countless shadings in dreams and nightmares, that
was nonetheless constitutive for me. It is my first day of class at
the elementary school, and my great-aunt Berta Zeballos is accompanying me on the tram; we travel almost thirty blocks
from the area around General Paz toward Alberdi. Her hand
does not let go of mine, but there comes a moment when she
must leave me. The boys and girls are already lined up in the
courtyard dominated by the *palo borracho,* waiting to enter the
classrooms; when my great-aunt leaves, I still have not joined
any of the lines. I do not space myself at one arm's length from
the student in front of me, nor do I advance toward the classrooms with the rest of the children, I do not belong to any of the
lines, I stand apart and finally remain alone while the rest of the
world disappears inside. One of the teachers notices me and
asks me my name; I am not on her list; she calls to another
teacher, but she does not have me listed either; the word "reg-
istration" dominates this confusing exchange until, finally, common sense compels one of them to add my name to the list in
her folder. By pure chance, I am enrolled in a grade, in a section:
when I enter the classroom, lagging behind the others, the students are already perched upon their stools, rigid, perhaps swal-
lowing their terror just like me, or their amazement, but it is
only my own terror that seems to matter, the mark that is left on
me that will endure until this visit after my return from exile. I
am not on the lists, and this condition has been neither enno-
bling nor degrading but, simply, formative.

Or

Phenomenology

I t was rather unexplainable how the sporadic pages I would write wound up being called erotic texts. Even when they did not so much as graze the amorous question but followed the flow of other motivations, my writings would return to the erotic; they contained a sense of slowly floating in a thick syrupy substance, or, shifting over to the sign of air for descriptive purposes, it was very difficult to breathe within those texts, and, little by little, as I wrote them and later read them, I found I was closing myself into spaces from which I had difficulty escaping.

I have always felt that my relationship to writing and to literature in general was not one of total commitment; to tell the truth, I have not aspired to dress myself in that kind of clothing or to enter that literary dressing room, although, paradoxically, it is there that I have earned my bread and butter. Still, reality has endeavored to refute this assertion: the books I read suck the marrow and emotions from my bones; in the moment that I am reading them, the world that is revealed to me, little by little, subjects me to its laws and takes power over me.

Phenomenology

It is not the story itself contained within these literary works that transports or unhinges me, when the book so merits, but the atmospheres into which I plunge without having sought them. I do not remember what I have read, it is erased from my awareness from one day to the next, and I always have to return to the beginning in a costly back and forth of time and attention. The books I have read I could say I have read as many times as the days upon which I have desisted from, and then resumed, my reading, with yet another supplementary deficiency or peculiarity, which is that I read books as if I were reading them aloud, which results in even more hours of reading. So it can be surmised that I have read many fewer books than would be supposed for someone who has chosen literature as her predominant field of interest.

I take a book, for example, a book on philosophy that I have committed myself to read as an intellectual challenge, and I am convinced that I will be unable to endure its complexity, but I persist, I turn the pages back and forth, backtracking as often as necessary, and, stealthily, the book invades my entire self as if, through unknown arts, it conformed perfectly to my being and illuminated, with what would have been unimaginable potency before beginning the process, my understanding. Thus, gratified and fulfilled, I consider myself in possession for a short time of the universal knowledge that the book was supposed to confer upon me, but the more I feel invaded by the book, the more spiritual richness I seem to have accumulated, the less I can succeed in *reproducing,* even for a fictitious partner in conversation, what the book contains. The sensation of knowing, the illumination of knowledge, has been ephemeral for me with respect to books; nonetheless, I do not draw denigrating conclusions from this fact: to tell myself, for example, that I simply do not understand would be a false inference because the wisdom of the book hurls me into zones of true revelation as if carried upon a gust of wind, even if later I return to a narrow field of understanding.

Condemned to maintaining a secret, almost confidential, relationship with the works of intelligence, but unable to take advantage of them as instruments for argumentation or integration in the world of ideas, I confine myself to letting the intellectual matter deposit and decant itself into my being, even though it might only represent the slightest of sprinklings, with no other intention than to feed on the warmth that it radiates. In deficit, my intellectual appropriation proceeds by mouthfuls; but when I try to bite into the entire mass, the individual parts evade me; when I concentrate on the parts, the mass becomes indistinct, and thus I feel my way along, releasing or grappling with what I can take hold of, barely storing away the dregs of the great cauldron.

I have tried, at different moments in my life, obliged by circumstances, to insist upon certain exercises of an intellectual and formative character, and the results have never varied: when I endeavor to obtain knowledge, some distraction, something like the song of the sirens, draws me away from the formal ways in which knowledge is usually forged upon the mind, and I seem to embark upon an impractical route, and what I should read in order to gain knowledge becomes increasingly blurred, while what lies to the side, above or beneath a text, without hierarchical positions, begins to assume a certain clarity and brilliance, driving into the shadows the information that constitutes the knowledge to be acquired and transmitted. The interstitial, a second or third skin of what is written, diverts me from the crux of the matter, and what I know, that which I propose to understand, is not something I can exhibit as an acquisition or even as an intellectual accumulation. Correlatively, my recall of what I have read, what could be the interchangeable material for a dialogue with a specialist in the field, is circumscribed within a censored forum: even if I wanted to make a show of recalling some fragment of a novel, or reciting verse, I would certainly flounder in a jumble of stammering, or I would end up speaking of one thing while believing I was speaking of another, in a dangerous sort of mental block with no way out.

All of this has been a handicap for me because the universe of formalizations has manifest handholds to which one must cling, and if one latches onto the wrong one the whole construction collapses, or is converted into something else, and one is left increasingly exposed and unprotected. For this reason I have tremendous admiration for the qualities of so many intellectuals, both men and women, who express their ideas, sculpted with strokes of intelligence, following a development and an order that has become evident to them through a practice of the spirit and discursive experience, and I find I can spend hours delighting in those faculties that I myself lack.

In order to survive in the world of literature, which, for reasons of career and profession, has been my world since I was very young, I at first made a great effort to acquire the most up-to-date instruments, those that would have permitted me, had I obtained them, to give classes, direct courses, lecture, do research, and all the other aspects of acquiring and imparting knowledge that are germane to the literary field. I did not give up on the undertaking, and during my exile I initiated, together with a number of friends, the reading of *Phenomenology of Spirit,* by Hegel. Those volumes, translated into French by Jean Hyppolite, had fallen into my hands thanks to the advice of an expert; in a Paris bookstore, I asked this person what book he would buy if he only possessed the few francs that I had and was planning to get along without any other book for the next thirty years. He was not surprised by the question; he listened to me as if I were asking about what style of suit or dress I could buy that would last for the next few years without going out of fashion. He answered, firmly: *Phenomenology.* And he also recommended a voluminous text of commentaries by Jean Hyppolite himself, causing me to spend all the money I had with me, thinking, perhaps, in terms of thirty-five years' worth of reading.

I began to read and to traverse the thirty years with my Mexican friends. We read the French translation and, more or less simultaneously, the Spanish version published by the Fondo de Cultura. We would read from the two books, and then we would turn to a third, the commentaries by Hyppolite. Our sessions would begin at four in the afternoon on Mondays and at seven on Wednesdays, leaving the book to rest from Wednesday to Monday, four days to return to the book at any moment in order to corroborate a point or just to exercise our minds. Of the three of us, not one possessed any particular knowledge, we were as naive as we were unpredictably astute, thus suddenly, with no competency for assimilating the text, we each came to believe that we understood everything.

The text would alternately evade and deliver itself to us; there were readings that we would enter and exit like dolphins in the sea, rejoicing in the immersions and acrobatics, convinced that we were grasping absolute truth; but at times the selected frag-

ment was like an unscalable cliff from which we would slide and
fall into stupidity and emptiness. The text was really *something
else*, it was a kind of drug that lifted us and gave us wings to fly;
phrase by phrase, we took hold of the words materially, and, by
what mysterious power I do not know, those words, beyond the
concept they contained, mesmerized us in their mere pronunciation and produced in us a profound sorrow. During those afternoons we passed from one ravine to another on a great mountain
slope, and the substance that we were touching was the pain of
discovery. We had not gone beyond the first fifty pages of *Phenomenology*, not counting the remarks by Hyppolite, before those
sessions became, I believe, our personal and customized cere-
monies for the intense revelation of the Spirit, a "philosophic"
epiphany after which we were able to arrive, in a way that was
unrepeatable, at understanding, or *an* understanding.

The task of weaving, that is, constructing a design by interlacing
the threads of the weft and warp on a loom, or that of needle-
work and embroidery, has a tendency to be equated with writing. The comparison falls flat quickly, however, unless sustained
by other arguments. I suppose that what links the two tasks is
the fact that weaving, like writing, can be taken up in various
and isolated places, unlike other activities. There is a certain degree of abstraction in the labor with textiles such that during
the time dedicated to weaving, it might be said, the person disappears and no longer exists as a being in the natural course of
time; what is captured in those moments of separation or distancing is a vibration far removed from the world, an almost imperceptible sign that only serves as a reminder that the world

exists but that the weaver is now far away. The body is crouched at the loom, the hands pass back and forth, from right to left, the fingers separate the warp creating openwork, the gaze traverses the fabric from one point to another, and a series of signs reveals the presence of the weaver and his or her dedication to the task. Still, the weaver is not there because the act of weaving the design has transported the person to another dimension that has nothing to do with the action being executed, although it may be its consequence. The labor, however, remains; it is the result of a voyage over the warp, but what has taken place so that the yarn should occupy the void and construct the fabric has no relation to any "reality."

In the same way, one does not write or paint what one sees, hears, smells, or feels, nor does one write in the place where these actions of hearing, seeing, or feeling take place; it has always been a hurdle for me, and, in a certain sense, for many years, a paralysis, to admit the separate nature of the dimension in which writing and weaving take place, labors that I have carried to their conclusion, the first with less commitment than the second, during the period of exile.

Those secret and uninhabited compartments, those no man's lands where one finds oneself when one wishes to write, or when one wishes to discover and understand a text such as *Phenomenology,* differ from the paradises that are brushed against through the textile flight; they are, just as I struggle to characterize them, of opposite signs, because in the realm of the textile there is a kind of joy in nonbeing and of nonlocation, whereas in the textual (where one arrives through writing or thinking) one only encounters misfortune, and not misfortune as a personal sentiment, but as an expression of fundamental nudity: not knowing, the inability to fill the void or approach the universal.

Those texts that have the power to put one in such a state of risk can all be counted on the fingers of one hand, especially when the reader is someone like me, <u>who has read so little while reading so much</u>. The notion of nudity and vulnerability is not produced by an entire book, nor by a single chapter, but can arise from a single sentence, and not even a sentence, but in the sediment that the phrase leaves behind in its wake, in the fragrance that is left by its passing, and that is precisely what I have gathered and gather from my readings, the reduced awareness of having been cornered by the text in an "absolute" situation, although this word has a very high referential cost.

During my exile I wrote erotic texts, but not because I was trying to write them; they planted themselves on the paper and came together quite on their own, without my having to summon them. Sometimes they were stories, and almost always they were simply narratives and were not written as one writes literature, just as we did not read *Phenomenology* as if it were a philosophic text. If at times I write about art, I am not an art critic, if it occurs to me to think in political terms, I do not think that makes me political, if I weave on a loom, I am not then an artist; I do nothing, then, to be brutally honest, I am nowhere, and the only place where I hope some day to return is that place that became a reality, instantaneously, when three surreptitious friends began the thirty-year reading of Hegel, and that place must be the place of the Spirit.

Exposure

A man lives and sleeps in the plaza. He scarcely ever moves more than a few meters, never outside of a thirty- or forty-meter radius. He has no pressing engagements and sees me walking my dog every day and surely cannot imagine what effect the simple awareness of his being there has upon me, nailed to his decision to live exposed to the elements while I move about my house, my balcony, or my terrace, while I go about the city, taking buses, walking, or hopping taxis, so close to him and, sometimes, without his even seeing me, only ten or twenty meters away, in a vehicle or on foot, without interrupting my routine or disrupting his decision to brave the elements; he is there, seated on his bench, facing the sunrise every morning over the Pizzurno Palace, turning his back to the sunset over Paraguay Street in the direction of Riobamba in the evenings. He is seated on his bench, and if he gets up at times, it is to inspect the garbage can that hangs from a tree or to lean against another tree and urinate (which is his landmark, facing Callao Street); it is obvious that this distraction of taking a walk is transitory. He will go back, he will not leave his spot.

Exposure

On the tenth of February, 1988, he was there. Sitting on the right side of the bench, he was crouched over and writing in a notebook, some kind of album, laid open across his knees. The eleventh, twelfth, and fifteenth of February he was there, writing on his knees; between seven and eight in the morning he watched the sun rise over the trees of the plaza, writing and greeting the arrival of the day, and it might be supposed that he had already fetched water from the water fountain, a squalid trickle, as I later discovered when this man began to interest me and I had contrived to investigate his most elementary means of survival.

For a week I saw him peer up over his glasses but twice, his absorption in his papers was so sustained, so constant, that nothing could divert his supreme interest from what his hand was writing so close to his head, as if this man thought with his eyes and believed that, the closer the paper came to them, the more conviction he would invest in the material of his thoughts. His ideas spilled upon the paper detached from his arched-over body, submissive to the laws of gravity, and, free of resistance, the writing appeared to organize itself into imaginary lines.

I sat on a bench not far away, observing the framed scene of the man with the vast forehead, prolonged by a baldness that reached back to the nape of his neck, with long strands of hair dangling to the sides as often occurs with that type of baldness when the one affected does not try to hide his condition. This framed scene, the tableau including the man, had been difficult for me to capture, as the surrounding benches were not always unoccupied, and, in addition, I had to consider my own position at a distance from the park guards because of my dog, whose entry was prohibited by a municipal ordinance, and my dog is not

Exposure

an easy dog to inconspicuously control as he pulls on the leash, excited by imaginary prey, reenacting the archaic hunting rites of his species. Day by day, I observed this man through February and part of March, and I was always on the verge of asking him who he was, what he was doing, the reason for his circumstance as writer to the morning sun, the golden star, and gradually my curiosity became an obsession and went on through those long months, except that the obsession passed through perfectly defined stages, as if it were fashioning a structure all its own from variables of an intense emotional and sentimental diversity.

I pondered different ways to approach him, and as the most appropriate quickly became frayed and meaningless, I never managed to formulate the question that would have properly recognized the poignancy and drama of the situation. It never seemed normal to see that man on his bench in the mornings stretching out before the arrival of the day, and it was even less acceptable to see him covered by an enormous plastic sheet on days when storms devastated and flooded the land and in the plaza where gusts of wind and rain caused no less confusion and mayhem for the passersby. Those storms, looming over the roofs of buildings, rising from the river in giant waves and hurricanes, beat against the windows of my tower and poured streams (increasingly like rivers) of water over the interstices of my poorly sealed windowpanes, and I spent hours mopping up the puddles that formed in the living room with rags and towels while the man had only his body with which to fend off the unleashed eye of the storm.

Much as I strive to maintain the chronologies, I grow weary trying to remember the precise dates on which transpired the instantaneous variations in the life of the man of the plaza ex-

posed to the elements and to establish when the changes occurred in my relation to the scene he dramatized. The record,
I always told myself, should have been maintained daily, but the
idea of a meticulously kept diary in which I would note my
observations of the man seemed to be of a grandiloquence and
of a pretentiousness that seemed inappropriate to the circumstances. Only now, several months after those events, can I try
to put them in order through writing.

I was often alarmed: one morning I saw that only *his things*
were there (a suitcase of red-checkered canvas, a box, some
stuffed plastic bags, a blanket), but not a sign of him; scanning
the horizon, from the corner of Rodríguez Peña and Paraguay
Streets, there was not so much as a trace of him, I could not
even entertain the possibility of confusing him with some other
pedestrian; nothing, I saw no one, much as I tried to distinguish
him, he would not appear, only his belongings remained in the
middle of the mini-scene, his park bench at the center-of-the-
universe, all exposed to the cold air amid swarms of pigeons
that swooped down upon mountains of bread crumbs, and the
obstinate persistence of my gaze combing the park from tree to
tree, person to person, from Charcas to Callao, without taking a
step because only by remaining motionless could I retain in my
mind this place that I knew to be the man's and survey the area,
so exceptional due to his absence. I left without having discovered him, after circling the entire periphery of the plaza, examining it from all angles and discarding in a dizzying fashion, one
by one, the many presences my eyes lit upon. Along Rodríguez
Peña I walked as far as Charcas, where I turned left as far as Callao, and then again turning to the left I walked over to Paraguay
and passed behind the bench, which at first in my uncertainty

had seemed to be at an approximate distance of one hundred meters but which was now barely five meters away; I could see that not only was he not there, but I also confirmed that he was capable of absenting himself and leaving his things in the care of God while he went some place that his public life did not permit me to imagine. I crossed Paraguay, advancing toward Rodríguez Peña, retracing my steps, when, turning the corner with the intention of going all the way to Córdoba, I came face to face with the man; he was walking in the middle of the sidewalk and we almost collided; he proceeded down the street, crossed the plaza on a semidiagonal, and reached his bench. In order to witness these movements, I situated myself at a fixed point, pretending to be distracted, attending to my dog, until I confirmed that he was again seated on his bench, had recovered his papers and lifted them onto his knees, and that his writing was once more spilling from his head, through his glasses, and onto the page.

On summer mornings it was necessary to get a start on things much earlier so as not to allow the invasion of the heat, the people, and the traffic to dominate one's world and inhibit walking and even breathing. The beginning of a day in Buenos Aires is like a waterfall crashing toward a sluice; neither the cold nor the heat, neither the wind nor the rain is protection against that gradual and suddenly complete saturation of the environment, and what is unleashed and multiplied until reaching legion proportions seems to have an awareness of its own cycle, to have a consciousness of its own rhythms of expulsion and retention, like a biological organism. The year is like that, the seasons are like that; the middays, the afternoons, and the nights are nothing less than the profuse and desperate response of that legion or

the Alan
Bennet
Lady ... car
story.

Maggie
Smith.

that mass to the climatic laws and, paradoxically, the uncon-
sciousness of finitude that it persists in maintaining. In those
minute-by-minute cycles, which are really hour-by-hour and
day-by-day for any mortal being, the man of the plaza's position
in the universe could not be, logically, equal to that of everyone
else's. To live the life of exposure to the elements affords neither
the satisfactions nor the deceptions of what one either accom-
plishes or fails to accomplish over the course of time; in that
state of exposure there are no concrete or practical chores, no
small closures that block off periods of time; contracts neither
begin nor expire, there is neither a time to leave nor to arrive,
one accumulates neither profits nor losses, there are no long-
terms, short-terms, or medium-terms, highs or lows, one does
not travel along routes with checkpoints, one does not have to
pay tolls or to pay one's dues; it would be endless to enumerate
all the things that have no end, all that does not have to be done
and that has no place in the place of exposure.

I was afraid to approach him; but around the middle of February, I began to think, not without some distress, that the misery
of my isolation corresponded to my growing and obsessive concern for that man. Upon awakening, having just detected the
emptiness in my solar plexus, the similar emptiness of a person
in my bed, and the ferocious breaking of the day—I must say,
Dylan Thomas's advice to his reader has always seemed misdi-
rected to me in the verse that says: "Rage, rage against the dying
of the light"—I began my strategy of small "endings" and new
beginnings, fundamentally laid out in precise chores to be carried out one after another, voraciously and ferociously, over the
course of the day. Doing things is a way of life; this may seem
obvious, but it is not so obvious to people who fold and unfold

Exposure

their existence as if it were made of paper and then go on folding
it smaller and smaller until there remains only a thin scrap left to
stand on. And then such people undertake just the opposite
process, opening and closing and opening yet again, the task begun becomes the task concluded, the day goes by, between periods of marinating and cooking, periods of waking and sleeping;
the time spent waiting for the sun's passage from one angle of
the room to the other and the decision of whether to follow it or
evade it: whether to spread something out wide or fold it up
thin, to attenuate the anguish, and nothing more than that. But if
there are no chores, if the folding and unfolding is performed on
the basis of pure being and the absence of doing, contact with the
universe will necessarily be stark and withering. And thus I imagined the course of the man's day, his mind merely concerned
with his own progress over the page, removed from the foldings
and unfoldings of daily life. That is what I supposed, but what
was really happening was quite different because, inasmuch as he
might have believed that he had escaped from such minor goals
and concerns—the greatest goal was, as yet, unknown to me—
he was submitted to inescapable routines; to go from the bench
to the garbage can, from the garbage can to the squalid drinking
fountain, from there to that place that was still unknown to me,
and to return to his bench, embarking on erratic trajectories
around the perimeter of the plaza as if looking for something,
probably dropped cigarettes, and not much more than that, over
the course of the forty-five minutes of my observation.

Another shock administered by the man in the park was in
fact an illusion, the kind that sometimes occurs to me while observing the streets; I find myself swimming in a semiconscious
state of flotation, and I see things that are really not there. On

[122]

Exposure

this occasion, I arrived at the plaza at quarter after seven and walked for about fifteen minutes, having noticed that the man was still sleeping. I walked around the plaza in counterclockwise fashion, then turned back and went around again, this time walking clockwise; I walked around yet again and the man went on sleeping. It was already eight o'clock in the morning, and the noise had grown intense, horns were honking, birds were chattering, there were rackets of all kinds, the scene was dense with both humans and animals busy at their assorted tasks: strolling, meandering, taking a turn, gathering, running, stretching out, people walking their dogs, others, like dogs, accompanying people. In the restless city the man went on sleeping; he could be dead, I thought, or perhaps deep in his dreams, or maybe sleeping off a late-night hangover, or exhausted from weakness. When I entered the last stretch of my around-the-block sequence, almost at the end of the lap, drawing close to the famous bench with the sleeping man, I suddenly saw him coming across the plaza on a diagonal as if from Paraguay and Rodríguez Peña; he walked along with agile steps, though he looked somewhat tired and worn, which is his own rather contradictory posture, recognizable at a distance: he walks pretty much like any healthy mortal, but hunched over. On the bench a man, some other man, went on sleeping, but he, my man, went over to him and destroyed, in one swift, almost arrogant gesture, my entire idea of the scene by snatching the blanket away—we were already at the end of March—and dismantled the form of the man who lay beneath, he made him disappear right before my astonished eyes and set to folding up, meticulously and carefully, with geometric precision, the blanket and other elements of his bed, perhaps a second blanket, an oilcloth, that had served as a base, and some clothing, and after he had folded up all his possessions, he put them into a bag and sat down on the bench.

Through February and the first two weeks of March, before the storms, the man must have survived the dog days of summer by refreshing himself with no more than the trickle of water from the public water fountain or, perhaps, one or another morning ablution offered by the sculptured woman who, nude and leaning forward, poured a minimal thread of water from her pitcher, barely forming a puddle in the fountain's basin, and whose waters did not always flow. The rains on those sweltering and humid February afternoons, when they occurred, must have been a blessing for the man; at the first drop the people would scatter and race for cover while he took refuge, paradoxically, among the sheets of rain, which was the key to his solitude and self-sufficiency.

It occurred to me then that perhaps the park keeper, who had whistled at me that first day when I entered with my dog and who had since left us alone out of sheer inertia, may have had some information concerning the man, though I could not ask him because he would have brought up once again my violation of the municipal code; I also thought that the neighbors who leaned from their windows along Callao and who observed the man's movements, and nonmovements, day after day might have wondered about him and have forged illusory explanations regarding his situation, even more illusory considering the limitations people have these days with communication, the fears people have of never shaking free of someone having once communicated with them.

Those who cross the plaza every day, and even those who carry out certain tasks in the plaza, would not consider approaching a man seated on a bench who, in addition to being presumed a *bum*, was perhaps writing a book or a musical composition on his knees, and thus the satisfaction of curiosity would have to be postponed in favor of endless speculation. I could not see what the connection was between that man and the others who were living their lives exposed to the elements: there was an *elderly gentleman,* of some sixty or more years, in a full summer suit, including a tie, who had made his home on a bench in mid-February and who sometimes produced some fruit from a bag (always a bag, the bag is the great signifier of the life of exposure), a bunch of grapes, for instance, which he would wash, one by one, under the trickle of water at the drinking fountain from which, previously, the other man had drunk, who, for me, was the *principal man* of the plaza due to his unwavering determination to live beneath the open sky with neither roof nor shelter whatsoever, and after washing the grapes he would eat them, picking out the seeds, which, as part of the prodigious cycle, he would offer to the pigeons or other birds, which, in turn, would go very nonchalantly to drink at the fountain: that gentleman, all suited up in the summertime, and even more so in the autumn, had a cardboard box of considerable proportions that he carried, with some difficulty, from one bench to another; one day around noon, I saw him on the 109 bus, we both got off at Montevideo Street, and he made his way with his box toward his spot, stumbling on various occasions because the box had no handle, nor did it have enough of a handhold to enable him to carry it on his shoulders, but, nonetheless, there went the *secondary* man, intent upon carrying his cargo. A few days later I saw that this secondary man had deposited his box below the principal man's bench, which revealed to me the fact that he, in fact, operated a kind of collective storage center where all the bums could leave their bundles. I often thought of William Kennedy's *Ironweed,* but I did not have the novel with me so I could not compare the situations of these indigents in the Plaza Rodríguez Peña to those of their brothers in Albany, New York, and I was only aware of the great challenge, an inner fierceness, that convinces one living the life of exposure of the relevance of his acts, which guides him in his daily movements, in pursuing those ephemeral goals from moment to moment.

My interest in the man of the plaza would put me, whether I wanted it or not, in an exceptional state, if not one of urgency; it inspired a literary emotion in me, in the broadest sense, of the kind that one feels when one comes across a forceful revelation in a text concerning the question of being, and this revelation, erected as a kind of limit, expands one's sense of vulnerability and sharpens one's perception of death, one's awareness of death. The first few pages of this story, before I begin to speak about the man in the plaza, are closely related to my return to Argentina; they were written in Buenos Aires, almost always beginning at ten o'clock in the morning and resumed after my walk in the plaza, returning with an exhausted, yet relieved, dog, and they were taken up again in Mexico, during a two-month trip; but suddenly, my writing ground to a halt, faced with my concern for the man in the plaza. I was unable to continue because this sudden interest of mine obliged me to choose among legitimate states of personal paranoia so as to avoid confusion. I did not know what my own situation of exposure was, and I could not know, therefore, what his was either, and, furthermore, this interest in his presumed decision to live exposed to the elements was offered to me so aptly for transference onto paper that I became suspicious, not wanting to convert the exposure of the man into a literary theme when my decision had originally been to use the narrative as a catharsis devoid of all vanity.

Nor was I hoping to discover the supposed key to the theme, the overused picklock to an infinity of narrative doors; I did not want the man, consequently, to become a theme, topic, or, much worse, an object. In spite of these restrictions, often, while in the plaza, I sensed the text flashing through my mind as if a growing impulse were taking power over me at the very pit of my stomach and over my disposition toward the written word, pushing me, almost imploring me, to put into writing this notion of metaphysical extension produced within me as I beheld the certitude with which the man folded his sheets beneath the tree and, overall, the charged silence that surrounded the bench when he, head down and bent close to the paper, set himself to the task of writing; the scene demanded to be written, all I had to do, in my turn, was to lay some sheets of paper on my knees and let the words that came from the man, framed in his location, spill onto the page; the pitiless clarity of that image arrived prewritten, yet I refused to translate it.

I do not know whether these exercises of control, of my writing over that man's writing and his exposed condition, were demands of purity, but I needed to know, through a selective chemistry, what kind of message the man in the plaza and his circumstances were sending and in what way it should be attended to given my own circumstances, having just returned to Argentina. In that situation of vulnerability, which parts were his and which parts were mine?

In the plaza, as the end of summer was drawing near, on a bench close to the spouting sculpture, another man installed himself, a third man, quite definitely a hobo, one whose flesh had been blackened by the charcoal of poverty, as if covered by the ashes of the embers of other times, his stomach bare to the air, his fly wide open, and with a very noticeable limp. The man had succeeded in isolating himself in a private conversation, un-interrupted, a self-responding soliloquy, self-sustaining, accompanied by the gestures that generally lend emphasis to all dialogues and communication between people. This man did not deposit any bundles at my principal man's storage center; there did not appear to be any relationship between the two men, but it was neither valid nor defensible to investigate one of these men to the exclusion, for no particular reason, of the other: they were both bums, but it was very clear to me that the main object of interest for me was not the man who viewed himself as a focal point, who included himself and only himself in his autonomous conversation, but the other man, who put his ideas on paper. For the one, the man who let his words drip onto pages laid across his knees, I had a predilection, for the other, or the others, only a pitying perplexity. One wrote messages, the other allowed himself to be conquered by the madness of pure gesture, condemned to a treadmill of solitary communication.

Monday, the seventh of March, at half past seven in the morning, I decided to approach the man. It had rained intermittently during the night, as if the rain were bestowing its blessing on the end of summer, and he had finished his ritual of unfolding and folding, piling and sorting, and he had begun to write on his papers, scribbling on the second or fourth line of a page when I interrupted him and without preamble inquired if he was a writer. He had already lifted his head when he saw me coming along with my dog, and also without preamble, as if it were per-

fectly natural that I should stand at the door to his abode and in-
quire into his activities, he answered that, strictly speaking, he
was not a writer but that he was writing about certain pending
problems, mathematical questions that he had proposed to himself some time before and that he was only now resolving. I told
him then that I too did some writing and that he had interested
me because I always saw him writing so early in the day. Perhaps
I should have asked about his living situation, exposed to the elements, but I did not; he took charge of stating things as they
were, "I take advantage of my circumstances," he said, "to make
progress toward the solution of certain theoretical problems."

"The circumstances in which I find myself" was the way he described his situation, having one believe that they were transitory. That same night, as if to intensify still more the emotional
tumult I had experienced upon speaking to the man in the plaza
for the first time, laying bare the paucity of communication, the
vulnerability of the words he and I had spoken, and the vacuity
of the link that they had established, it began to rain ferociously,
and by midnight the storm had become even more severe, with
thunder and lightning and thick curtains of rain lashing against
the buildings and sudden illuminations along the charged and
fantastic horizon. I have always imagined during such storms
that I am on a ship and that the storm is hanging overhead and
then bursts over the mast and sails, and this ship is a simile for
the stormy and emotional life of a novel being read or a poem
being murmured like a prayer before the shipwreck destroys
everything and leaves terror in its wake. And that midnight the
man in the plaza made sleep impossible for me, I was conscious
that life outdoors, exposed to the elements, was the supreme inclemency.

Exposure

It rained all night and continued raining throughout the following day; on the night of the second stormy day, my crisis of conscience had advanced: how could it be that, having had an apparently normal conversation with the man in the plaza, everything would now go on the same as before? I will just have to accept, I told myself, that nothing will be the same, that having spoken to him and having learned of his circumstances, I was now in a difficult situation, no doubt about it, because if I was able to speak to him there, outdoors, then there was no apparent reason why I could not do the same in the living room of my own home, because to have it any other way would be to establish certain hierarchies in my relations by discriminating among the subjects of my attention.

The fact that the exclusive focus of my attention at that time in Buenos Aires should have been reduced to that solitary man and his brief excursions seemed very significant to me and open to various fashionable interpretations. It frightened me: the dialogue had been opened and could not be closed, every day the quota of interchange had to be fulfilled without fail. Once verbal contact had been established between the protagonist of the plaza and me, the incidental passerby, I necessarily found myself in a state of dependence, I was converted into his tributary, and because he had *chosen* to remain exposed to the elements, performing his mathematical abstractions on paper beginning at eight o'clock in the morning and continuing through the day, I felt relegated to my place beneath an oppressive and incarcerating roof, living under *house arrest;* my "production" and the completion of my supposed text were trivial domestic chores next to the enterprise of this pillar of a man.

Exposure

Around that time, one afternoon, at the bus stop on Callao, there appeared a strange man, a freak of the city; his distinguishing characteristic was that he pointed at people with his index finger, poking them in the back or the chest, as if trying to get their attention; on this occasion, he pointed at me, and I did not know how to react. I realized he was an exceptional kind of person and that my reaction would have to be abnormal as well. At first I tried to ignore him, but he would not quit, he kept pointing at me, jabbing his finger into my ribs just above the abdomen. I was filled with terror and very confused and could not respond to the man's questions, spoken in a kind of jargon all his own with a meaning that was incomprehensible to me; the freak moved away, and nobody in line, waiting for the bus, lifted a finger to defend me, not even to comment on the episode; I felt completely alone: everybody went on staring into space, and, instead of exercising my rights of citizenship, so to speak, standing up and demanding to be heard, which always helps in reconstructing one's damaged self-image, I felt ashamed at having been subjected to the finger of the freak, in front of such haughty and indifferent people who, in their silence, made me pay for a double or triple sin: that of having placed myself within range of the man's finger, that of not having been able to efficiently handle his behavior without experiencing terror, and that of not having been able to inspire any kind of collective response in the face of the assault to which I had been subjected. Noticing my anguish, only one woman among those standing in line was moved to say anything: *He's completely harmless, don't be afraid of him, he doesn't do anything, he speaks that way and pokes his finger that way, but he won't do you any harm.* Then she added: *You know,*

Exposure

it's genetic, whenever anyone in his family reaches adulthood they begin to make those noises and to make those signs with their fingers. His mother ended up the same way, his brothers are like that too, they all do the same thing.

Do you live around here, señora? I dared to ask the woman, seeing that she spoke of the freak as if he were a member of the neighborhood. She told me that her mother had a stall in the community market between Córdoba and Viamonte, stand number forty-five, she told me, but I immediately forgot the number, and after that I always tried to remember whether she had actually said forty-five or forty-nine every time I went to the market in search of her mother. I went in search of her because I went so far as to ask the woman in the line at the bus stop if she might know, by chance, a man who lived outdoors in the Plaza Rodríguez Peña, a man who was constantly writing. She said that her parents, in particular her mother (the woman at the number forty-five stand, now a widow), had gotten to know him quite well at one time, him and his family, and she went on to tell me that he was also totally harmless. *Ah! That one, yes, he's harmless, he spends the whole day writing; he was an advanced student of technology, almost an engineer, to the point that the children bring their physics and mathematics problems to him for help and, yes, he solves them. He is totally harmless,* she went on saying, thoughtfully, and I let one thirty-seven bus go by after another, and she did the same, because we were talking about something that interested her, something that seemed to her and to me to have something to do with our lives. Indeed, she told me, *people said that he had ended up that way due to a trauma,* that his parents had died in an accident he had survived and that he had never recovered from the blow.

Exposure

Finally, we got on the bus; I was perturbed because a few moments before she had commented to me, in a tone as if to lead into a subject of even greater importance, that Olmedo had killed himself.[1] She must have interpreted my blank expression as a sign that I had already heard the news, but when I asked her who Olmedo was, she looked at me, aghast. *What?! You don't know who Olmedo is?* she said. The punctuation signs of admiration and interrogation blended one into the other. *No,* I said, *I don't know who Olmedo is. Olmedo, Olmedo,* she insisted. *The actor, the comedian, he threw himself from the eighth floor of a building in Mar del Plata this morning. Ah,* I told her, *Excuse me . . .* , and once again caught in my perpetual stream of apologies, I began to explain my past; I told her that I was not really from the area, without knowing how to explain that I was from there and yet again I was not, *what is here? what is there?* I felt like describing for her, with emphasis, the relativity of these concepts of belonging to a certain place, but I only succeeded in confusing us both: *I'm from here, but I was born in Córdoba, and all these years, besides, I haven't been in the country, I was living in Mexico, and really I'm from Mexico, too, or I prefer to be.* She could not believe what she was hearing; *don't be afraid,* she told me, and perhaps she thought that I was totally harmless despite not knowing who Olmedo was. As the hours passed following that episode, I became increasingly aware of just how much of an intruder I really was, to what degree I was a foreigner in this country: the suicide of Olmedo dominated the Argentine landscape, it saturated the press and

1. Olmedo was a well-known television comedian whose controversial death was considered by some to have been an accident and by others to have been a suicide.

the media, no one spoke of anything else; the magnitude of my ignorance seemed to leave me washed up on the banks of the world. But I was in possession of data concerning the man in the plaza, I knew that he was there due to the effects of an intense trauma, just as the woman had told me at the bus stop; he was totally harmless according to that woman, who seemed to measure the dangers of the city in terms of the damage that certain marginal people might be able to cause. I have gone to the market on numerous occasions searching among the stalls in the series beginning at forty-five, which was the number I thought she said, up to forty-nine, but I have not come across any widow, the stall keepers are all men; they do, however, sell cheeses and cream, like the mother of the señora. A few weeks later, the man in the plaza, in his commentary of the day, mentioned that at times he would get a carton of milk at the market, and I was on the verge of asking him if the señora at one of the stalls from forty-five to forty-nine had given it to him, but I resisted the impulse because I would have had no way of justifying knowing about the stall keeper or knowing about him through the señora's daughter; besides, he had said that he bought the milk.

I learned that the man in the plaza, my principal man in the plaza, was named Andrés. I told him my name in turn, which, over the course of several weeks, he systematically distorted, changing the first n of my name to a t, and I never corrected the error; it has been a long time since I last corrected the errors people commit with my name, they no longer affect me or put me in a bad mood, and I believe, I am convinced, that they are simply harmless mistakes. A t in place of the n, an i substituted for a u, an o in place of the first u, etc., these things do not upset me as they used to; I now know that this is my name, there are no more doubts as to the identity that the name confers upon me, but this was not always so; there were times when I did not know how to respond, pressed by the insistent inquiries of the curious who wanted to know the name's origin, its meaning, and at times I would find myself truly disconcerted when assailed by questions for which I could give no answer. With Andrés, it did not seem appropriate to clarify that the second *u* in my name did not precede a *t*; I preferred to put my trust in the possibility that some illumination in another context would dissipate this particular flaw in our relations.

I have already spoken of the gesticulating ashen-colored man: with wide and varied movements of his hands and arms and even his whole body, as I observed one morning, he would direct an imaginary orchestra in which the instruments were his own voice. These concerts would begin after nine o'clock in the morning. I asked Andrés if he knew who the man was, if to his knowledge the man had some "transcendent" relationship to music. He did not know, did not seem at all curious about his fellows, and I had the impression that just by asking the question he must have suspected that I had some literary and unwholesome curiosity, so I did not insist, still not being in a position to explain to him what my relationship to literature was. He only told me that an ambulance once came and took the man to the hospital for an infected foot, but later he was returned to the plaza. "But that one is from the other side," he said, the *but* emphasized the distance that separated him from the other man. This type of declaration he would repeat on a separate occasion when a sinister old woman, carrying a cane and dressed in rags, passed close to us and bowed reverentially toward him. "She must have been a servant," he commented, "because she comes and asks me for the shopping list for some kind of banquet, as if I were her employer. When I give her what she wants, she goes away, satisfied, *to the other side.*"

With Andrés I proceeded with great discretion; I could have deluged him with questions, trying to learn at all costs what had made him choose his way of life. It was not necessary to lay siege to him: what he was willing to give did not constitute what could be called a narrative body, in a certain way he, with his scarce references, eliminated any specialized interest and obliged one toward asceticism; to his extreme privation of material goods, there could only correspond a maximum austerity of demands; with him, nothing could ever accumulate. Nonetheless, in spite of accepting these rules for dialogue, in the days that followed my first conversation with him, I was in a permanent state of conflict. I isolated the different states of my consciousness, extracting all humanitarianism from them, but that was only a mental decision. As the various natural phenomena were unleashed upon us—rains, winds, freezing cold, lightning-filled nights—he became more firmly entrenched on his bench, and his defiance brought me closer and closer to impotence. He who was so clearly on the limits of human potential had rendered me incapable of understanding his defiance.

Besides speaking to me of *his circumstances*—a word that defined, as I indicated earlier, a certain transitory nature—he told me that he had been living that way for four years; previously, he had lived in the plaza in front of the Medical School, a few blocks away; one day he had been forced to move, on the advice of the park guard: the police had been carrying out antidrug operations in the plaza, and the guard did not think it was a good idea for Andrés to expose himself to all of that. It is impossible to know whether or not the guard was really just tired of imagining how this solitary man survived the storms, the heat, or the invasions of mosquitoes, not to mention hunger and other necessities, and perhaps he just preferred to breathe easier by getting rid of him.

I asked him once if anyone had ever taken an interest in his circumstances, for example, someone from the government, one of the so-called social workers from the Ministry of Welfare. Nobody had ever approached him with any other intention than an aimless curiosity, a bit like my own, but in my case it had become more and more of a crisis of conscience, not to say a profound spiritual conflict. Sitting there beside one another on his bench I knew that the others, the passersby, the people, any observers who saw us there talking, would be calculating the incongruity of such a meeting: a woman, a dog, and a man who was one of the principal features of the plaza, somehow fitting into the hierarchies of the homeless; first me, the woman, then the dog, and then the man. That same day that I wondered whether we were being noticed, he told me, as if divining my thoughts, that he believed that *his people from other times* were perhaps watching him live this way, and I had the impression that knowing that they were watching him was a kind of triumphant confirmation of his undertaking. There was not even the slightest evidence of the trauma referred to by the señora in the line at the thirty-seven bus stop.

No, he was not bothered by anyone or anything. The wind on those hot nights undoubtedly did him good, listening to the birds at dawn was nothing to scorn, nor was there anything wrong with enjoying the autumn sun. Nonetheless, he did not seem to express much appreciation for nature in our conver-

Exposure

sations. The din of the birds barely allowed us to hear what we said to each other, and I heard myself saying to him: "I imagine the birds wake you up." He told me that some time before he had read in a magazine that a bum in New York had chosen to live on the streets because his wife "had birds in her head." "The two of us have birds in our heads; in my case, they wake me up, in his case, he runs away from the birds that inhabit his wife's head." It was the first time he had used the word *bum*.

I have never been able to describe him or define him as a bum. An unexplainable prohibition deprives me of that word, it is driven away from me like a bad omen. In contrast, after my first meetings with Andrés, I entered a kind of conversational delirium. I would tell the whole world how I had met him, I wanted at all costs to transfer the problem to others, and, grossly, I have to admit, I tried to exorcise him through the mere act of describing his circumstances. To people without scruples, pious people lacking a sense of humor, hateful people without a sense of love, opportunists, apathetics, to all of them I told anecdotes related to "my friend Andrés, the man in the plaza." I was miserable, miserable for so much time; to the highest bidder I would sell Andrés's truths and mine, but, suddenly, without the mediation of any event, or perhaps it was just the tedium, I stopped babbling. Since that day no one has asked me what happened nor have they referred to that erstwhile daily babble. It has been easy to preserve in silence the figure of the principal man of the plaza ever since.

We spoke of literature offhandedly; he was interested in Rulfo; he said he had read *Pedro Páramo* some time before and had the feeling that it was a great novel. I told him that before he died, Rulfo could be seen walking the streets of Mexico City,

Exposure

along Insurgentes Sur or the southern stretch of Revolución, that anyone could cross his path in the streets of San Ángel and even exchange words with him if they wished. He noted my having clarified *before he died,* as if to distinguish between the walks Rulfo may have taken after his death.

He told me that he had two books. One of them, whose importance he discounted because it was a novel by Blasco Ibáñez, he had found in the garbage together with a large number of other books, all cookbooks, *imagine that,* he said, *to find a bunch of cookbooks, what a paradox.* Some fool had thrown the books away, and he had rescued only one. He took the book by Blasco Ibáñez from a canvas suitcase and showed it to me without comment. The second book was *La novela de Perón,* by Tomás Eloy Martínez. He made it clear that it had been given to him as a present but that it was an abridged version. When I asked him if his edition contained a scene in which, by a pure coincidence of fiction, my husband, my son, and I appear on a balcony, while below there is a political demonstration taking place and the music *Oh, Solitude!* by Henry Purcell can be heard, he said no, that if that scene had been in his edition he would have remembered it perfectly because he knew almost everything that happened in the book by heart. Intensely and accurately, and considering it a veritable interpretative discovery, he remembered Tomás Eloy Martínez's idea of a reality perceived through the eye of a fly: multifaceted, contradictory, and of unknown dimensions; *I believe,* he added, *that's how it was in those times, a hodgepodge.*

During the month of March, Andrés must have attended, against his own volition, the demonstrations of the teachers who were striking in front of the Pizzurno Palace, the seat of the

Exposure

Ministry of Education. They berated the minister, they complained, they demanded en masse the right to gather as they
literally filled the plaza and threw thousands of flyers and pam-
phlets into the air addressing all different problems and con-
texts. At dawn, the plaza was covered in papers that the wind
lifted and whirled about or that the rain soaked in irregular
mounds. No one swept up the remains of the teachers' rallies.
The strike was going to be long and the sit-ins repeated, such
that any sweeping up would have been futile; the plazas, because
in fact there were two, a large one and a small one, divided by
Rodríguez Peña Street, were almost always filthy and were now
dunghills littered with the soggy, papier-mâché-like mounds of
flyers strewn everywhere on the ground.

I imagine that Andrés felt obliged to put up with the invasion
of the demonstrators and the garbage, given that he never commented on the events that had taken place on so many evenings
before our meetings in the plaza for the last few weeks. I do not
even know if he was well-informed about the conflict that was
taking place within the confines of the plaza and that he saw evening after evening. He heard, surely and without a doubt, the
slogans, but when I offered to bring him some newspapers, he
refused to accept them. He preferred not to know what was going on in the world. I had never known anyone who, so con-
sciously and decidedly, refused to hear anything about the news.
It was impossible to talk to him about what was happening; he
could not be consulted on, nor had he even heard about, this or
that event in such and such a place whose effects had had these
or those repercussions; he could not be involved in what was
happening, which restricted enormously our resources for conversation. It is enough to imagine what would happen to two

Exposure

people, or several people in a social gathering, if they should decide not to speak about what had appeared in the newspaper and only to exercise the use of words that go straight to the point, without tangents or euphemisms.

Speaking to Andrés became increasingly difficult for me, to interest myself in the ways in which he organized meteorological events seemed ridiculous; I could no longer tolerate asking him about his way of life, his *modus periendi,* as Gonzalo Celorio, the Mexican expert in the ways of street people, would say, and often, like a coward, I went to the plaza too early, avoiding the meeting and limiting myself to watching him as he slept, wrapped up like a tamale in his blankets, resting his head on Tomás Eloy Martínez's novel of Perón.

dreamlike

The Wall

The sun bears down, unrelenting, upon the walls of the house throughout the day, until night falls over the earthlings, usually around eight in the evening, ending with the first light of morning at about five, but at this latitude the sun is eternal. Not even the slightest breeze is blowing, or, as they say in my family, "not even a drop of air is blowing," a qualitative exchange of properties that makes the air seem even thicker and condenses, without precipitation, the desire for rain.

The force of the sun cannot be neutralized: the narrowest of openings is an enormous gap through which the sun's beams filter and disperse, scorching, glancing off all surfaces, and radiating blinding gusts of heat. At the roots of one's hair, in one's pores, at the very foundations of the body's cells, the vapors seethe upward, and it is impossible to control the demand for water that these incandescent states provoke in the human substance. A tropic without palm trees swaying, without the relief of plump round drops pounding the earth and filtering through parched cracks, without desert mirages to unite sky and earth in a blue horizon, with none of that, a tropic such as this, vibrating in pure whiteness and flashing like a sword striking against the edge of all things, is a condition of the spirit: all is dense, the broth does not clarify, nothing flows in the nucleus of exhaustion, and the wall that faces me, the medial wall that rises from the ground floor of the building across the way, reaching to the twelfth floor, is both my doom and my incitement: nothing can bring it down nor diminish it in any way, it is there, demanding in its solemnity that the optical illusion become reality and the dream become fantasy.

The gray of that wall, whose dimensions are not those of just any back of a building, persists, it is not bedazzled by the beams of light, its grim dry tones are much more akin to my emotional condition than to the raging January inferno. Never on one plane have the vertical and the horizontal achieved such equality, never has the idea of the extended surface been so well laid out, comparable only, perhaps, to a great plain, a steppelike canvas, a smooth mantle spread over a reality upon whose tension the entire spectrum of light is displayed. Back, ribcage, hip of a structure in the heart of a city block, it looms upward from its concrete foundations like a cliff and defies the aerie from which I peer outward, staring at its mass. My vantage point, as viewed from the wall, if someone were to observe it, would appear as a narrow mountain refuge in the still cool shade, waiting for the sun to cross over the vast dividing chasm to begin its pitiless assault. Between my wall and that other wall the space is deep and wide; darkness descends into the shaft, a sheer vertical drop where a whole mysterious world lies beyond my reach, perhaps of tiled patios upon which water flows freely, without loss to evaporation, some greenery here, some cave flowers there.

The heat possesses, the sun dominates every breath and ob-

The Wall

liges an economy of the body: to remain, to store, to linger in
the dead time of the interminable siesta, and to only permit the
mind to review brief passages of reality, this is the discipline that
one learns. Thus, static, confronted by pure wall, sandwiched
between these walls, in this lodging purloined from the ravine,
suspended and imprisoned in a niche at the limits of the abyss,
only my index fingers stroll across the keyboard, romantically
interpreting the link between this landscape and my soul. In this
gesture that passes from intense black to transparent brown,
from burnt sienna to moist earthen, or that dissolves and re-
forms in shades of dirty browns and shrouded whites, there is a
resistance that silences the terror and contains the madness. The
slower and more somber the action on the keyboard, and the less
interrupted its course, the lesser the risk of its precipitation.

As I explore the back of this wall in the heart of a city block
and climb it like the human-fly without taking hold of its pro-
trusions, through pure adhesion, victorious over the abyss, I accept the silence of the surface that denies me its history and re-
futes all anecdotes, my index fingers seem to perceive, but the
gist is evasive, they believe they are sculpting, but the striations
are blurred: there are no interpretations in the desert, the sun
devours and engorges, for only the sun can process what happens on the vertical-horizontal plane. But patience offers a possible vision: to wait until the afternoon sun warms the back of
my neck and releases the last strand of my hair and, then, to observe the delicate manner in which the sun engraves the moment upon the giant screen before me, whose desirable and distant swirls I myself sketched without realizing it, or that I
anticipated at the rosy walls of Morelia, on the rusty rocks of the
citadel at Besançon, on the worn bruise-colored rocks of Aniza-

The Wall

cate. My mountainside, my urban mural, receives the colors of red as if it were being attired for a sacred ceremony, and then, with the first drops of air, it slips into darkness.

From my window I have been attentive to the variations on the witness-wall. That it should have been my backdrop, or that upon that backdrop my return should occur, was an accident of "construction": I could just as well have sunk my roots in Buenos Aires in an eight-by-eight cubicle, with a balcony facing an avenue and a line of witness-trees or witness-buildings with dozens of windows all fortified with shutters or billowing with curtains; I could have returned to the interior of that small box I occupied in the sixties, in whose hollow of light still resonated the voices that were silenced by terror in the seventies; I could have stayed in one of those two-story buildings in the *barrio sur* with vast rooms and walls that disappeared upward to the ceilings, peering into the streets from an angle, as if pleading forgiveness from the surrounding buildings. All of this could have come to pass, but when I saw the Dover cliff sunk into the heart of this city block, as vast as my own heart and as white as the Wailing Wall, when I saw that gigantic movie screen upon which the scenes of this new beginning were to be projected, the explosion of reds on that late afternoon drove away the panic I felt before its very immensity.

I was returning to an all too familiar cave in the city, and in its creation certain unchallengeable emotional verifications had taken place: in 1984, in that first month of my stay, I had laughed and cried alternately and unstoppably like a child during a night of catharsis. To laugh in one's own country is more powerful than to cry, and more powerful still is to laugh after crying. It was necessary to take a stand in that rediscovered condition, to

make a nest in that hollow in the cliff across from the wall, to go
from the sky to the earth, to soar over the city, and to even accept its deceptions, which I would have to discover for myself,
unaided.

The wall had previously appeared in my Mexican dreams surrounded by high clouds, and the minaret where I was to sit later
observing the wall, that chamber I had chosen for overcoming
those simultaneous outbursts of laughter and tears, was a small
refuge adorned with plant-covered balconies affixed to that concrete mass where I sat staring at the changing tones of the wall-
mountain-witness subjected to my observation and interpretation. For weeks upon weeks I remained facing that rampart,
and, in that walled garden of sorrows where the sun and the
shadows would spar, I would deposit traces of myself, airborne
in this case, since of my own volition I did not once set foot in
the street.

One might suppose that I sought to find an oracle there, that
deciphering the signs would lead to some kind of calling. But no,
I allowed myself to be swept along by the coloration of the atmosphere, the direction of the wind, the meteorological events
and other environmental specifications that, for me, have always
been the augurs of our existence, and the wall seemed impen-
etrable, a hurdle between me and my descent back to earth.

On my first night of coexistence with the wall, once I had sur-
veyed its base from what was to become from that moment on
my private terrace, once I had confirmed the wall's perimeters
and evaluated its diameter and radius, which surpassed the
norm for any typical medial wall, what really struck me was that
nobody could possibly scale it and that, inasmuch as running
away was quite impossible, other methods of escape would have

inasmuch in Spanish?

to be found, by subterranean means or by passing overhead. I once saw a helicopter circle the wall and then, after two or three skillful dips, disappear on its way to the port; and *from a distance,* as literary signs are so often perceived, I heard a ship's siren, and its sonorous blast conveyed a profound sadness to me on my observation and listening deck: one would have thought that my condition of immigrant had summoned it deliberately, like a melancholy solace. Under the spell of the evening's serenity, I decided to slip down a tube: I was determined not to let myself be disturbed by the emotions of the rediscovered city. But my intentions were thwarted; first, I discovered that the wall at its heart, and the block that was to be my dwelling from that moment on, the site where I had thought to live out the second half of my own private century, alternately laughing and crying according to my moods, was in fact at the very center of the city and that walking a few blocks to my right was the La Paz café, legendary for its intellectual meetings in the fifties and sixties and for the hunting of people in the seventies. But I was in for a surprise: personally, I had never kept a single appointment there, but generations had made it their fantasy bar, and now complete strangers returned to the scene of the crime like bees attracted to honey, and the thick cloud of smoke betrayed the suction and expulsion of their anxiety.

I never knew the real Corrientes Street; it was one thing to have walked along it as a stranger, recently arrived from Córdoba, and even when I was living in Buenos Aires I maintained a certain distance from it and felt that sweet sense of estrangement that compelled me to see it as an object of desire; but this new perspective after fifteen years of absence was quite different: the image that occurred to me, setting sentimentality aside, was that death had gained mastery over the place. There was one point in my favor: never having had either a historical or ideological attachment to that street, I was afforded a pristine response to its summons; if now, upon my return, it overwhelmed me to envision the absentees in this street, or to perceive the absence of those who were no longer there, it was a kind of symbolic tribute to its agglutinative and mythological function. My memory did not choose to recall anyone in particular but, rather, offered a kind of restorative evocation.

I chose Corrientes. I selected that street over other promising avenues, and I walked the blocks that encompassed my neighborhood; I have always been parochial, limiting my movements to the area in which I live. I walked from Callao toward *el Bajo* breathing deeply of the fresh March air, almost always in the afternoons with my back to the setting sun, but always with enough time to witness its final descent on my way home and also with enough time to catch the reds of the sunset on the wall outside my nightly refuge. I chose to return along the parallel streets and at the perpendicular intersections; I would see the edges of the city, a distant blue vertical view, sometimes green, but always serene. There was not much more than color to see on those promenades; but one day, on the cross street between Corrientes and Córdoba, the stretch between Tucumán and Viamonte, to be exact, I began to pick up familiar signals; I had walked this same stretch every two or three days for the last three months and nothing in particular had happened, but now, suddenly, I found myself on Reconquista Street, in front of an enormous building of many floors that bore the name of an important firm; there were some broken walkways, and, through the concavity of crystal in which an image appeared, distorted

[148]

and grotesque, I saw light flashing from the panels of a revolving door. On the corner, a classic old restaurant-bar emitted odors of Spanish cooking and nothing more than that, no other details were forthcoming in that first vision of the street. In that street, which I had not acknowledged in all those months, I had worked for several years: it was a newspaper office that I had left, that many people had left, and in which many others had died during the great repression; and that was the bar where the dead and the absent would go; and that was the street and the corner where I waited, daily, for the bus to take me home, and it was, above all, the corner at which stood Rodolfo Walsh's house, his building, where I would go every day and which, now, possessed by a great and instantaneous sense of recovery, I entered solely to commemorate the advent of my return to Buenos Aires. At the bottom of those steps I once again sensed the pursuer at my back, but Rodolfo was no longer there to open his apartment door for me, to conjure up, with his malignant wit, the paranoid reflex. This meant, I reasoned, that the elements had become volatile for me over those last few weeks, that a sector of the universe, of history itself, of consciousness, had stopped functioning with all of its reality-based attributes, that I had fallen victim to a selective and repeated aphasia because the erasure had not been produced on one single and innocent occasion but, rather, every day, and the revelation, as I find I must define it, had not been spontaneous but had been provoked by a simple commentary, by someone who was with me at the time, with respect to the odor of garlic that emanated from the restaurant. The involuntary escape from a space that, on the other hand, had been a point of reference insistently reproduced in my memory during the years of my Mexican exile brought to light

the conditions of my return. It was also a kind of somatic projection that integrated all the other symptoms circulating
among the many personal histories: to suffer an attack, to gen-
erate an ulcer, to go blind, to border upon tachycardia, to suffer
dyspnea, to break out in a rash, and even to perish so as not to
see, recover, or remember. With more conviction than ever I set
myself to the task of no longer fleeing from anything, no longer
avoiding the abyss, nor passing over it through cunning, and,
above all, from that moment on, I no longer trusted lucidity or
wakefulness.

I tried to visit the last house we had lived in, an apartment
building with a wide corridor on the ground floor that ended in
an enclosed and murmur-filled garden. There, the fragment of
reality had inescapable force; but I could not grapple with it for
other decidedly traumatic reasons: I wanted to visit my old
house, but just as I was arriving at the corner of the street, just
drawing near, I experienced a terrible sense of panic, not in the
chest, curiously enough, but in the back, and I returned home
without having been able to carry out my mission. Little by little, I started to eschew that area of the city, expertly avoiding
the site with circuitous detours. But everything comes to pass,
and, so, one morning, I got out of a taxi right at the front door,
I went all the way back to the garden, and quickly came back out
along the corridor. The scene I recaptured in that moment was
in no need of explanation: I had not imagined a relaxing visit,
like taking a child gently by the hand, nor an energetic maternal
excursion to run errands, but an attempt to escape in which I
came out of the elevator, started walking toward the exit, and
there I saw coming toward me three well-built, recognizable
men. I pass by them, and as I go out I see that they are speaking

delusional

The Wall

to the building manager in the rear, at the entrance to the garden; the manager directs them toward the front door, right toward me; I manage to see them out the back of my head, as can only be done by those who know there is no escape; nonetheless, I still try: I cross the street and flag a taxi; just as I am getting in I feel two hands grabbing me by the shoulders and holding me back, forcing me to return to the house. I try to get away, to wheedle my way out of my predicament by offering to take the stairs while they take the elevator, I even propose the inverse, but they have me cornered. In the garden, stamped against the light in the background, looms the figure of the building manager.

Vertigo felt at one's back is worse than the attraction of the void, it is the magnet of the unknown, a mouth sucking one inward by the heels, against the current, and at the same time hurtling one forward. Behind one's back are consummated both the betrayal and the coup de grâce, and it is enough just to concentrate one's thoughts intently upon that, to separate oneself from oneself and to perceive there, at one's back, that one is totally defenseless.

The reflection of light from the wall hurled white darts directly into my eyes, and the windows could not be left open; early in the morning I closed the blinds and reinforced them with blankets in order to contain the darkness; those days I took refuge on the other side of the house until the sun shifted and punished the other side too. Relief only arrived at about eight in the evening: the air began to circulate through the house, entering through the windows, lifting the edges of the curtains. Those breezes provided the closest thing to relief, sudden gusts of fresh air granted isolated states of well-being, but the sense of

The Wall

privation was so severe that I would feel grateful for those fleeting moments. I sincerely believed that the condition of being alive could be a kind of voluptuous state of grace, so long as I knew how to wait for the end of the day and to put my faith in the sign of the air, suspended upon the surface of the wall, with sufficient energy to radiate from there through my windows and into my rooms.

I believed in circulation, but there were some wooden nickels circulating in that space. One evening, having gone out on the terrace to take some clothes down from the line, there was an immense cockroach on one of my garments, a lustrous dripping species of vampire clinging to the fabric with such strength that even flinging it with violent desperation would not make it let go. Finally, I managed to shake it loose and I went back inside; I was trembling with terror, my teeth were rattling, great heaving sobs only served to remind me of my struggle on the terrace, I was beyond consolation. As much as possible, I forced myself to calm down, I turned off the lights and sat in a chair, trying to disappear, to remove myself from reality. I cannot say for how long I remained in that condition. When I thought I had recovered my ability to breathe normally and my sobbing had subsided, I turned on the lamp and returned to life. With my right hand I inadvertently touched a wet, smooth object that scuttled from my thigh to my knee. The cockroach was living on me, it had attached itself to my body like desire; the trembling started all over again and, with it, my madness. I threw the creature away from me, and it grabbed hold of a curtain, its antennae waving from right to left, backward and forward, and its eyes staring at me from a distance, watching me as if waiting for me to let down my guard, waiting to return to my lap. I slowly

anxiety.

The Wall

backed away, trying to erase myself as a living being, to disguise all signs of life: I neither breathed nor blinked an eye, my slinking was my escape, first toward the other side of the house, then, once out of the creature's line of vision and far from the powerful range of its antennae, I scampered out the front door and dove headlong down the stairwell.

It was well into the night when I returned from walking on Corrientes Avenue; I had been reflecting upon those extreme states of mine and had decided to defend myself. This just cannot be, I told myself, that the cockroach should win, that the heat, the wall, the fear of heights, all of them should win the game and deny me my rights. In the elevator, taped to the mirror, there was an announcement that said, "Tomorrow, after eight o'clock, the exterminator will be in the building." In the upper-right-hand corner was a drawing of a cockroach and the name *John Killer & Co.;* as if compelled by the executioner's name, I carried out an act that felt like a crime; I wrote, clandestinely, beside the name, *Gregor Samsa,* exposing myself to discovery and condemnation. When I opened the front door and turned on the lights, the cockroach had disappeared. After searching every nook and cranny, I closed the doors and windows, blocked all the entrances, and hid myself in my room. The cockroach was still somewhere, but if I remained calm, without breathing, it would not approach me. From that night on, I shunned all sinister evening breezes.

Only stoicism could explain my survival in a corner, protected from insects and the heat by the subterfuge of shrinking into insignificance: the less bulk my existence denoted, the less the possibility of my being noticed. My reserves were sufficient: a decision not to call anyone, not to ask anyone for anything; to respond to all who needed me, but not to complain; to expose myself as little as possible to all negations by others in order to ban the frustration of unfilled requests; to counteract desperation by relieving myself of all expectations. I achieved what, in my imagination, I had often created: a situation of confinement in which the awareness of available goods and of their being rationed by droplets assured a vital economy, a triumph over waste, an accumulation out of pure necessity and strict desire, all attributes that, for the first time in my life, situated me at absolute zero. I had to read the inscription on the wall: aureate stains of sundry sizes distributed around its center, droplets splashed in colonies in the upper-right-hand corner, elongated star-shaped crowns, markings engraved like short and long bars of code; smooth and absorbent textures prepared for engraving and, above all, for penetration, beyond and within the surface in which to lose oneself with the gaze and with the mind. Without passing over the wall, but maintaining myself in the pure wall-condition, I had to conquer the wall and extract a key image, one that shot out over its entire length and breadth and in every dimension at once, to take power over this image as if it were knowledge itself. But the silence was absolute, everything I hurled against it rebounded or slithered down without leaving a trace among the eternal markings, and then this deciphering began to resemble more and more one of my crazy undertakings: one that I would construct in order to insist that reality reveal its reality.

In small, awkward letters, in the upper-left-hand corner, I began to write. The pen scratched the surface and then moved forward with an uncertain line, producing small clusters of text. It darted ahead spewing slashes, then entangling itself in *s*'s, but

The Wall

could not break away from its nuclei; as if the terror of the un-limited surface were conditioning it, it went about creating areas of reserve, leaving a trail of bait as points of reference to which it might return in case it got lost. The scroll began to fill up in various directions, with texts and overlapping texts, on lines and between lines, with blank areas and areas configuring representations beyond their own relevance; the pen rested on its point or lay on its side, it became an awl or a gouge but gave no indication of how I could avoid the ephemeral character of its incisions. I enclosed the smallest blocks within more blocks, and the distended page was soon crowded with nuclei surrounded by grooves that in turn were covered by stitches continuing out-ward without losing the initial form of the capsules, and the wall, overloaded by a violent energy, pierced and racked by graffiti, exposed to an inclemency heretofore unknown, con-strained by the chasm and dominated by a prolonged siege, be-gan to crumble, literally, upon the straight line at its base; it did not collapse and fling rubble in all directions, as a building might during an earthquake, but, rather, it slid down into the line at its very foundation, like a sheet of paper sliding vertically into a slot.

In the Latin American Women Writers series

Underground River and Other Stories
By Inés Arredondo
Translated by Cynthia Steele
With a foreword by Elena Poniatowska

Dreams of the Abandoned Seducer: Vaudeville Novel
By Alicia Borinsky
Translated by Cola Franzen in collaboration
    with the author
With an interview by Julio Ortega

Mean Woman
By Alicia Borinsky
Translated and with an introduction
by Cola Franzen

The Fourth World
By Diamela Eltit
Translated and with a foreword by Dick Gerdes

The Women of Tijucopapo
By Marilene Felinto
Translated and with an afterword by Irene Matthews

The Youngest Doll
By Rosario Ferré

Industrial Park: A Proletarian Novel
By Patrícia Galvão (Pagu)
Translated by Elizabeth Jackson

In a State of Memory
By Tununa Mercado
Translated by Peter Kahn
With an introduction by Jean Franco